YANKS IN THE OUTBACK

Dave Ives

A story of Woomera, South Australia, the Joint Defense Facility Nurrungar (JDFN), and the First Gulf War

Copyright © 2015 by Dave Ives
All rights reserved.

This book is a work of fiction.

Cover design by 100Covers

IVESGUY.COM

ISBN-13: 978-1511985246
ISBN-10: 1511985240

Table of Contents

Preface 1
Introduction 7
Part 1: Feb – Apr 1990 12
    Arrive in Woomera 12
    First Impressions 12
    One Man Shop 14
    First Day at Work 15
    Vegemite and the Cafeteria 15
    Sizing Up the New Guy 18
    Sammy Hard Act to Follow 19
    Sammy Leaves with a Bang 21
    Eclipse season message 24
    Eclipse Season; No Days Off 25
    Eclipse Season Briefing 26
    Eclipse Brief Delivered 27
    Printer Paper Delivery Service 28
    Eclipse Commanding 32
    Aussie Accent 33
    Command Failure 36
    Command Failure Fallout 39
    Command Failure Finale 42
    "You're a Cowboy" 43
    Military Ball: OK to Go 46
    Military Ball – Wrap Up 47
    ANZAC Day Article; Gibber Gabber 49
    Gibber Article Feedback 51
    ANZAC Day 51
Part 2: May – Jul 1990 53
    Lt Kelly Gets Decertified 53

Dance with Navy Girl 57
First Aid Response Team 62
DO is Leaving 64
Smoking Area Incident 65
HQ Data Request 67
Mud Stomping Incident 70
New Satellite Coming 72
Phony Australian Accents 73
Sammy's Girlfriend 76
They Call Me "Bluey" 77
IG inspection coming! 78
GSR: 1st Meeting 81
Independence Day Parade 84
GSR: 2nd Meeting 85
Capt Marcus; "The Great Escape" 86
New DO Arrives 90
IG Inspection – Hide the Books! 90

Part 3: Aug – Oct 1990 93
Eclipse Season – No More Mid-Shifts 93
Iraq invades Kuwait 94
What Team Do You Root For? 94
GSR: 3rd Meeting 96
US Troops Deploying to Saudi Arabia 98
IG Inspection: Are You Ready? 99
Brother's Wedding 101
Back from US 101
IG Inspection: Misplaced Priorities 102
Optimize Ground Station for SCUD 106
GSR: 4th Meeting 107
Pointer Program 107
IG Inspection: "We're here to help" 108

Ultralight Crash 115
IG Grade: Commander Scolds Me 116
Summary Courts Officer: Assigned 118
Summary Courts Officer: Done and Dusted 121
GSR: 5th Meeting 123

Part 4: Nov 1990 – Jan 1991 124

Flight 15 Launch 124
GSR Meeting: Are we ready? 125
Flight 15 – When can we see it? 131
SCUD Launch; Iraqi Test 131
GSR Meeting: Software Puts Best Guy on Job 132
Software: "We can't do it" 134
Software: "Show me the requirement?" 138
"I want you to complete the all commands test" 141
Letter of Congratulations 152
FLT 15 Comes into View 154
Lt Kelly Decertified – Again 154
Ohio State Loses to Air Force. 159
DIY Air Con Repairs 161
DIY Aircon II: Problem Solved! 164
GSR Meeting: All good; we're on the bird all the time 165
DIY Aircon III: No Good Deed Goes Unpunished 166
Desert Storm Begins: Air War 171
SCUD Launch on Israel 172
FLIGHT 15 – We're Taking Operational Control 174

Part 5: Feb – Apr 1991 175

Letters from the Front 175
Gulf War Not Top Story 177
Prayer Luncheon – Justifying the War 177
Not Bombing Civilians? 179
Baghdad Shelter Bombed 180

Damage Control 182
Lessons learned … not learned 183
Letters to the front 186
Going to the States 186
Ground War about to start 186
Russians Getting Involved 187
Traveling to LA 189
Arriving in USA – Ground War Success 190
Allied Forces Trouncing Iraqi Army 192
War Over 192
Victory Bug 193
Troop Support 194
God Bless Guam 195
War Victory Speech 197
Continued US Presence in the Middle East 197
Soldier's Welcome Home 199
AF Academy Boxing 200
Feeling of Patriotism 200
Not all Rosy on the Farm 201
Heading Back to Oz 202
Headquarters Wants Blood! 204
HQ changes the rules! 210
Capt Marcus Decertified 211
Dances with Wolves 211
Epilogue 215
About the Author 221

PREFACE

This story is fiction. But, it's based on my personal experience while stationed as a United States Air Force First Lieutenant at the Joint Defense Facility Nurrungar (JDFN), near Woomera, South Australia from February 1990 until May 1991.

All the characters are made up but most of them are based on real people.

Purpose

I have three major purposes for writing the book.

First, since the JDFN no longer exists, I want to give an inside look at what life was like when Yanks and Aussies were working and living together in Woomera. My story is a historical snapshot of life at the JDFN and Woomera in the early 1990s through the eyes of a young US Air Force Lieutenant.

Next, while stationed at the JDFN, the first Gulf War played out. The build-up, the air war, the ground war and the final Iraqi surrender all took place during my tour of duty. In February 1991, I started a "war diary" where I recorded my thoughts, opinions and observations of the war. My diary entries provide some insight into how the war looked from the perspective of one US junior officer stationed overseas in the Australian outback. Some of these entries are included, almost word for word, in this book.

Finally, I felt compelled to write this book after reading a Wikipedia article about the JDFN and its role in the Gulf War. Here's the wiki entry that concerns me:

> *During the Persian Gulf War it (the JDFN) managed to score a few positive publicity notes for detecting early launches of Iraqi Scud missile attacks; years later, a USAF assessment would emerge revealing that oversights at the base were partly responsible for one of the worst disasters for Coalition forces during the war, on 26 February 1991 when an Iraqi Scud missile struck a warehouse housing U.S. soldiers, killing 28 and injuring more than 100.*
>
> *The report found that ground operators at Nurrungar played a part in the tragedy, which the Air Force described as a "worst case combination of events"; these were in turn compounded by failures in the MIM-104 Patriot intercept system deployed near the Dhahran base itself.*

Source: http://en.wikipedia.org/wiki/Joint_Defense_Facility_Nurrungar

This is a damning statement. I feel compelled to challenge it. This book represents that challenge.

Diary Format

The book is written in diary form. I did this for three reasons.

First, I kept a diary while stationed at the JDFN. As I re-read my diary entries I felt they conveyed a fresh and exciting vantage point – someone in the thick of events as they happen. Someone who doesn't know how it's all going to end. I like this frame of reference and decided to use if for my story.

Next, writing in diary format gives me some incredible freedom. It allows me to write from my perspective - my flawed perspective. I can freely express my opinions. After all, it's a diary; I'm just writing down what I see, what I feel, how situations look from my point of view.

Finally, writing in diary format gives me latitude to get my words down in raw, unpolished form. The writing doesn't have to be perfect; it's not supposed to be perfect - it's a diary. This latitude gives me more confidence to write. I'm not bogged down by grammar, punctuation or any other English teacher rules and regulations. This makes the writing more fun and free-flowing. Not sure this translates into free-flowing fun for the reader ... hopefully it does.

Three Types of Diary Entries

Generally, there are three types of diary entries as follows:

Type 1: Real entries. When the Gulf War broke out, I started a "war diary." Some of these entries are included almost word for word.

Type 2: Remembered entries. These are based on real events that I personally experienced. For these I just remembered the event and wrote it down as if it happened yesterday.

Type 3: <u>Made up entries</u>. I invented these to facilitate the story line.

Type 1 entries give the story a reality kick. I wrote these back in early 1991 while the Gulf War was raging. They're raw and opinionated; not politically correct.

Type 2 entries add flavor. I had a blast writing these because they're mostly entertaining; mostly fun. They bring back fond memories of my time in Woomera. Their role is to capture the essence of what life was like when the Aussies and Yanks were living and working together in the Australian desert outback.

Type 3 entries really drive the main story line. These are what I call the "decertification" entries where crew members are officially reprimanded for performance infractions.

It is here where I use the most creative license. I was not a crew commander. I don't know the details of their trade. But, as the sole military satellite systems engineer – with an office adjacent to the satellite operations center (SOC) – I was privy to the "inside skinny." The crew commanders talked to me a lot. They told me their woes; their headquarters headaches; their frustration with the rules they had to follow. From these second hand accounts, I've come up with my type 3 fiction entries.

I use these type 3 fiction entries to weave the underlying story line; the main thrust of the book; the overriding lesson to be learned. It's a lesson the military should already know; one they've already learned from previous wars. But, the lesson doesn't stick. It has to be re-learned again and again. And, the learning period usually occurs at the start of any new war. And, it can be a costly lesson; a lesson where sometimes the fee is paid in blood.

The sad part is the lesson is so simple; so basic; so obvious.

Here's the lesson – when you go to war, you must make the transition from peacetime operations to wartime operations. They aren't the same. If you don't make the transition, you're in trouble; you're setting yourself up for failure; you're putting yourself at a severe disadvantage. You just might lose the war.

Unclassified

All the information contained in this book is unclassified. I was pleasantly surprised to find everything I wanted to include is readily available in the public literature. So, the fact that the JDFN was tracking SCUD missiles during the Gulf War is no secret. My concerns about "classification" were completely dashed after reading, *"America's Space Sentinels: The History of the DSP and SIBRS Satellite Systems"* by Jeffrey T. Richelson. Richelson's comprehensive book gave me the confidence to go forward with this project.

Remember, after this preface, you enter the "fiction" zone. A fictional story based on real life events; based in a place that was once a joint US and Australian operational military satellite tracking facility; based on people who really roamed the offices and hallways of the JDFN and the streets, homes, and pubs of an outback Australian village called Woomera.

Dave Ives
Alice Springs, NT Australia
February 2015

Introduction

I was cleaning out my closet sometime in July 2012 and found this diary. It's a record of my thoughts, feelings and experiences while stationed as a young US Air Force Lieutenant at the Joint Defense Facility Nurrungar (JDFN) near Woomera, South Australia from February 1990 until May 1991.

Prior to getting stationed "Down Under", I read a fascinating book; a book that captured my imagination; held me hostage to every word; struck me as genius; had me stapled to the pages wondering what's going to happen next.

The book is written in a very unconventional format; a format that promotes honesty; a format that delivers the story straight; a format that lets through the raw, raunchy and real. And, I felt this format is what gives the book its edge, its excitement, its sincerity.

Its greatest appeal for me is this; I felt like I was reading the unmitigated truth.

And, what's the reason it's so hard hitting? What's this special format?

Simple – it's a diary; written by a seventeen year old Navy recruit from Massachusetts. While serving in the US Navy on a light cruiser during World War Two, he kept a secret diary. Of course, keeping a diary was against regulations. But, he did it anyway. And, I'm sure glad he did. Now, we have a first-hand inside account of what the war looked like from the vantage point of a sailor as the US Navy fought its way across the Pacific.

The book – Pacific War Diary by James Fahey – was my inspiration for keeping a diary while stationed in Woomera. I had delusions of creating something similar to Pacific War Diary; an exhilarating firsthand account of a historically significant event. I figured I had a unique experience – a Yank stationed with the US Air Force in outback Australia. There has to be a story in there somewhere ... so I decided to keep a diary; a journal of my feelings, opinions, insights and experiences.

But, as I wrote in the diary, I felt somewhat dejected because my entries didn't seem very interesting; or very exciting; pretty routine stuff. But, I kept writing anyway thinking I may be able to use the material someday to write a proper book.

Also, some of the things I wrote were probably classified at the time so, like young James Fahey, I may have been breaking the rules.

All this led to my giving up on ever publishing the diary in its original-uncut form.

When my assignment ended, so did my writing. I chucked the diary in the closet.

Then in July 2012, while cleaning out my closet, I came across the diary. As I flipped through the pages and stopped to read a few entries I got excited. Somehow, over the years, the entries took on a much more interesting flavor. They were fresh, fun, factual and fantastic. They were real. They were from my heart. They were what I felt at the time. Right, wrong or ridiculous, it's what I was feeling, experiencing, seeing at that moment in time. As such, I started considering the possibility of publishing my diary – uncut; in its raw form; bare bones, ugly bulges and all.

Then the objections started floating through my head. What about some of my "bonehead" entries; entries that sound a bit goofy – maybe even ridiculous - now? What about some of the negative opinions I express about the military and government? What about when I mention some of my co-workers in less than flattering terms?

... all good reasons to stop the presses ... but not good enough.

The way I see it, my diary has become a sort of historical data point because it documents actual events that occurred when the JDFN was an operational military satellite tracking site with both Yanks and Aussies working side by side. It documents life at the JDFN and in the Woomera village from the perspective of a young US Air Force Lieutenant who was there.

Why not publish it?

Another compelling issue is the Gulf War. The war took place near the end of my tour of duty in early 1991.

My diary gives a unique perspective of the war. A perspective of someone stationed at a Defense Support Program (DSP) missile warning site supporting the warfighters in Iraq. The mission crews at JDFN detected Iraqi SCUD missile launches and provided near real-time warning messages to the battlefield. As the military satellite systems engineer, I was part of the team.

So, again I ask, why not publish it?

As far as classified information goes - I'm over it. It's no longer an objection. I researched the information contained in my diary and it's available for anyone to read in the literature. It's all out there. You can Google it. You can buy books that describe it; describe it in much more detail than I discuss in my diary. I guess it's similar to James Fahey's situation – 20 years after World War Two, his secret diary is no longer against regulations; it changed from the realm of "against regulations" to "hurry up and get that thing published!"

The story goes that James called his World War Two commander and told him about the diary. His commander read the shoebox full of loose paper and then gave James the feedback he was hoping for, "We gotta publish this!"

My diary may not be as adventurous as Pacific War Diary, but I think it makes interesting and entertaining reading for reasons as follows:

- It's a historical snapshot of what life was like while the Joint Defense Facility Nurrungar (JDFN) Tracking Station was in operation.

- It gives an account of the Gulf War from the vantage point of a young lieutenant stationed overseas in outback Australia.

- It gives some insights into the cultural similarities and differences between the Yanks and the Aussies as they lived and worked together in Woomera.

- It tells about my struggles with life in the military; dealing with the bureaucracy and red tape.

- Even though it's a diary, surprisingly, there are several story lines. These stories uncover a few "lessons learned" and may make useful reading for present and future military leaders.

Like James Fahey, I contacted my commander from Woomera and showed him the diary. And, just like James, my former commander became my biggest supporter – he said, "You gotta publish it."

So, here it is ... enjoy ...

Sean Mitchell
Former JDFN Officer and Woomera Resident.
Pelham, NH
USA

PART 1: FEB – APR 1990

Arrive in Woomera

2 Feb 1990 Friday

I arrived in Woomera yesterday. I'm on a 15 month assignment with the US Air Force. I just came in from Denver, Colorado where I was stationed since July 1987.

First Impressions

3 Feb 1990 Saturday

Woomera is a very different place; different from any place I've ever been before.

My first impressions are not good.

Last Thursday, when I arrived at the local airport, my sponsor Capt Sammy Jenks picked me up. I know Sammy from back in Denver. He was stationed over at Lowry and I was up the road at Buckley.

YANKS IN THE OUTBACK

He worked in our shop for about a month before coming down here to Australia

I'm Sammy's replacement. He's been here for almost 15 months and will be heading to a new assignment in the next week or so.

As we drove down the main road through town – Banool Avenue – I was struck by one thing – how dead the place looks! It's a ghost town; everyone's gone; where are all the people?

Sammy gave me his take on life in Woomera, "You wouldn't believe all the things there are to do here! Sometimes I have to turn back invitations cause there's so much going on; or I just turn them back cause I need to rest!"

I thought, "Is he joking? He sounds serious. He wouldn't kid about that – would he?"

As I looked out the window of the car all I could see was empty deserted looking buildings and blowing sand. All topped off with a burning searing heat from the Australian summer sun. The scene reminded me of the movie, "The Day After" where they dropped a neutron bomb that kills all the people but leaves all the buildings in place. I found it hard to believe there were any other life forms here but us.

I wanted to believe Sammy. After all, I'm going to be living here for the next 15 months so I better make a decision to like it. So, I will.

One Man Shop

4 Feb 2014 Sunday

I'm taking over Sammy's position as Chief, Satellite Systems Engineering. Important sounding title but it's really just a one man position working as the Air Force interface between the civilian satellite support contractors and the operational crews. So, I'm the Chief of myself; one man shop.

My shop even comes with an official three letter designator – DOA. The DO stands for Director of Operations; the A stands for analysis. All the other three letter shops have lots of staff members but my shop – only one person - me.

At first I found it a bit ridiculous working in "DOA" – the Dead-On-Arrival shop. But after a while everyone just gets used to it and it's no big deal.

I worked in the DOA shop back in Denver where we had 5 engineers. I got selected for the Woomera position for two very convincing reasons. First, I had two and a half years' experience in the shop back in Denver. And, second, no one else wanted the position! I think the second reason carried the most weight.

So, Sammy and I now share a very roomy two bedroom flat on the southwestern side of the village. The building is known as the "Pimba Flats." I'll have the whole place to myself when Sammy leaves next week.

First Day at Work
5 Feb 1990 Monday

Today was my first day in the office. Sammy showed me around and introduced me to just about everyone. I'm very familiar with the setup as it's similar to Denver only a bit smaller and less people. So, I feel fairly comfortable getting around.

Probably the most important place for me is the cafeteria. Now that I know where the hot water and coffee is located, I'm set! And, I discovered the instant coffee is free! Just help yourself anytime. So, I'll be making the trek to the cafeteria frequently to carry out the procedure as follows: Pick up a nice clean porcelain coffee mug, then dump in some instant coffee granules from the wall hanging dispenser, add some fresh milk from the pitcher and then swirl it all together with piping hot water from the red handled flicker nozzle. Now raise the glass to my lips and enjoy – YUMMMMM!

Vegemite and the Cafeteria
7 Feb 1990 Wednesday

By the way, there's another free item on the cafeteria menu. No, I'm not talking about tea; although you're right, it's free too. I'm talking about an Aussie staple. Aussie's can live off this stuff; it's the Vegemite Sandwich!

There's only one problem. You see, as of right now, I'm not a vegemite fan; I don't like the stuff. It's a black paste made from vegetable extract. It has a very strong unique taste; like a bouillon cube except spreadable.

But, that doesn't matter. The Aussie's would riot if you took the vegemite sandwich off the free menu!

Today for example, I witnessed a somewhat heated exchange. A US Air Force Captain (Capt), Jerry Purvis shot out, "How can you eat that stuff? Tastes like axil grease!"

Capt Purvis directed his disgust at Mark, who works for the APS (Australian Protective Service) and was happily assembling a vegemite sandwich.

Mark calmly continued spreading vegemite on top of the butter that had been previously lovingly spread on the fresh white bread. Then when Mark finished his masterpiece he looked up at Capt Purvis and asked, "So, you don't like vegemite, mate?

"No way – Hate the stuff!" Replied the defiant Capt.

"So, that means you won't be digging your grubby hands into the vegemite jar?" Mark asked while glancing down at the half eaten jar of vegemite.

"You won't catch me touching any vegemite jars!" Capt Pervis stammered.

Mark then looked up calmly at the disjointed Capt and just before taking a luscious bite of his vegemite masterpiece said, "Good, then there will be more for me!"

After a bit of snickering laughter from the other Aussies at the table, Capt Purvis turned and slowly walked away. Hopefully he learned a valuable lesson – don't disrespect the vegemite!

I certainly learned the lesson.

* * *

I feel at home in the cafeteria. It's very welcoming.

I think a description of this happy gathering place is appropriate.

The cafeteria is set up with rows of tables. I like this. It facilitates people eating together; you just sit down and before you know it there are people around you sharing a meal. It's a great way to get to know people; great for someone new like me; great way to build good relationships.

The tables are decorated with some very important items. These items appear every three feet or so and seem critical to the well-being of the site personnel, especially the Aussies. This decorative group consists of the following: One tin container - with lid – filled with white or wheat bread, one jar of vegemite, one dish of butter packets, and a salt and pepper shaker combo.

So, it's almost impossible to go hungry at the site. Even if you have no money, you can live off the free coffee or tea and the free bread, butter and vegemite! Most of the Yanks leave the vegemite alone, but they wouldn't starve. And, the Aussies view the free vegemite sandwiches as probably one of the biggest perks for working here!

So, life in the cafeteria is good. When the troubles of the day get me down, I can always stroll out to the cafeteria and have a hot cup of coffee and some bread and butter.

And, later on, I hope to learn to acquire a taste for vegemite. Why? Because when I watch the Aussies eat it they look so happy; so satisfied; so content. I want some of that!

Sizing Up the New Guy
8 Feb 1990 Tuesday

Sammy is leaving this Sunday. He's heading out on an early flight to Adelaide, then over to Sydney for the long leg across the Pacific to the USA.

Sammy is a great guy. I knew him from the old days back in Denver. He's a character. Always ready with a laugh, a smile, a joke; he's a person who makes you feel better; makes you feel important. After spending time with Sammy, my spirits are lifted.

And, he's also a sharp officer. He's well liked here. He's respected.

I can feel the elephant in the room as my co-workers size me up, "Who's this new guy? Is he going to be as good as Sammy?"

There's a feeling of doubt about my ability to live up to Sammy's standard. And, it emanates down from the big boss Lt Col French. He's the Director of Operations, better known as "the DO" (DEE-OH). At the morning meeting he directs all his questions to Sammy. As Sammy rattles off another sharp concise answer, the

DO glances at me as if to say, "See what I expect of my satellite engineer? You better catch on quick as I don't want to be training you. I expect you to hit the ground running and start pulling your weight right away. This ain't no training ground."

As I look around the morning meeting room I see the other sections Chiefs and they're all sizing me up too.

It's only my first week; I'm taking it all in.

Sammy Hard Act to Follow

9 Feb 1990 Friday

Sammy is going to be a hard act to follow. He is the big man on campus. Everyone seems to love him; even the ladies – young and old.

For instance, the ladies in the cafeteria treat him like he's their son. The other day one of the older cafeteria ladies – Shirley, I think is her name – greeted him something like this, "G'day, Sammy, how ya goin? Talked to Joanie last night and she says you were dancing up a storm at the disco. All the girls had to stand in line to get a dance with you; is that true?"

All that said with an Australian accent. Not sure how to capture the accent in print but it enhances the conversation and gives it special meaning that's a bit hard to describe unless you hear it live.

Then Sammy replies, "Well, shucks, Shirley. You know I'm just having a bit of fun, kickin up my boot heals, gettin to know the local gals. I'm not nearly as popular with the ladies as Butch; now he's the real ladies' man!"

All that said with a Southern accent. Sammy is from the Deep South – Alabama to be exact. And, let me tell you, the Australian ladies cannot get enough of his major league southern accent.

Sammy's not shy about his accent either. He kicks it in high gear and lets it ring out across the land. And, it's great.

I really like him. You'd be hard pressed to find a more likeable guy.

And, the crazy part, I'm from the deep north – New Hampshire. Yet Sammy and I get along like brothers. I enjoy spending time with him.

We've been jogging together nearly every day after work. We've had many dinners together over the past week. I never get tired of hanging out with Sammy. Wherever he goes, excitement seems to follow.

Sammy is an Air Force Academy grad, but he's always talking about his favorite college; the one he wished he graduated from; the one he cheers for during the college football season.

Sammy is a rabid Auburn Fan! How appropriate for someone from the great state of Alabama! You don't want to get in-between two people from Alabama when they're arguing over the Alabama and Auburn football teams. They're very serious about their college football; especially the rivalry between these two superpower programs.

I'm an Ohio State grad and we can get pretty nutty too when it comes to college football!

The Aussies have a nickname for Americans. They call us "Yanks." Normally, this is a term of endearment; not usually a bad word, but, it can be. It all depends on how they say it.

But, Sammy told me he had a hard time with this term when he first arrived in Australia; especially since he's from the South.

As he tells the story, an Aussie greeted him, "Hi Yank!"

Sammy froze for a moment then regained his bearings.

"Me, a Yank? No way," Sammy shot back, and then continued, "I'm no Yankee! I'm from Alabama! Them's fightin words!"

I had a similar experience. The first time an Aussie called me a Yank, I became flustered. "I ain't no Yank, I hate the Yankees! I'm a Red Sox fan!"

Sammy Leaves with a Bang
11 Feb 1990 Sunday

Sammy left today. And, he left with a bang ... a big bang.

He had a going away party last night – at our flat. I spent Friday afternoon with him making the alcohol run. We stopped by the "class 6" store and picked up both hard liquor and beer. The class 6 store is for US military and family members only and everything is cheap; cheap compared to what you pay at the local bottle shop. At least that's what Sammy tells me. I've never been to the local bottle shop.

When we got back to the flat Sammy showed me a special trick. He took two cases of beer and hid them in one of the bedroom closets. "That way, when it looks like we've run out, we bring out two more cases!"

I didn't really understand because it seemed like we had enough alcohol for six or seven parties. I figured I wouldn't have to get anything from the class 6 store for months.

I was wrong.

I attended the party in a very bizarre state; a state unlike anyone else there. I attended sober. I figured it's my house and I better keep an eye on it; keep things under control.

About one in the morning someone in the crowd called out, "No more beer, let's go!" Just then Sammy sprang into action. He darted into the bedroom and reappeared holding a fresh unopened case of beer.

He was a hero. The party erupted with cheers.

He got another round of applause about an hour later when he carried out the last case of "hidden" beer.

I stood there dumbfounded as I contemplated how much alcohol had been consumed in one evening; in one party; by only 25 to 30 people. There must have been some very inebriated people wandering the streets of Woomera last night and early this morning.

I witnessed some very drunk people. One guy was standing in the middle of our living room holding a beer. He looked very unstable. I thought something was going to happen. It did. He dropped his newly opened beer and the bottle smashed to pieces on the carpet. The foamy liquid shot out in all directions soaking the carpet with a big gulp of warm beer. The carpet seemed more than happy to chug down every drop and then start working on creating a nice beer stink.

The poor fellow who dropped his beer simply looked down at the shattered mess, then proceeded to hold out his hand as Sammy slipped him another fresh new replacement. The smashed bottle on the floor was totally ignored; it got the same reaction as if he'd dropped the beer cap instead.

I watched the whole scene in amazement. But, I figured as long as they were all pretty well behaved, I would just let things play out.

Then, almost instantly – as if on cue – everyone was gone. I looked up at the clock and it showed 2am. Maybe they all had to be in bed by 2 and that's why they left.

But, I was wrong. It didn't take me long to figure out what ended the party so abruptly ... we ran out of alcohol. They cleaned us out; we had no more beer backup; we were totally dry. As such, everyone left; why hang around if there's no booze?

I learned a valuable lesson. Want to clear out the party? Just stop the alcohol. Once the word gets out there's no alcohol, everyone leaves.

* * *

Sammy made his flight this morning but it wasn't pretty. He scampered in a panic grabbing his gear and running out the door. His ride was outside our flat beeping the horn for about five minutes before Sammy even started to open his eyes and roll off the bed.

From what I understand, Sammy's exit was a metaphor for his tour of duty down under; he worked hard and he played hard. He was well liked and respected by just about everyone. And, the Aussie's loved his rock'em-sock'em swagger and hard partying lifestyle.

I'm not sure I can I can live up to this standard. I'm not sure I want to.

Eclipse season message
12 Feb 1990 Monday

I just finished writing a message for work.   Lt Col French – the DO – told me I had to have it out tomorrow at the latest; it's going to the Wing. I ran out of time today at work so I finished it at my flat this evening.

"The Wing" is the next level chain of command located at Peterson, AFB in Colorado Springs, CO. They want to be kept informed of our plans for the upcoming eclipse season.

I'm pretty happy with the message. I spell out in simple language our approach; we'll command the on-board sensor thresholds to mitigate the effects of the sun. When the sun shines down the barrel of the satellite, it's difficult to pick up other infrared (IR) signals; like the kind seen from missile launches. And, that's what we do here. We look for missile launches. We see em, we report em.

Eclipse Season; No Days Off
13 Feb 1990 Tuesday

The DO was happy with my eclipse season message and authorized its release.

He also seemed happy to inform me that Sammy used to go into work every evening during eclipse season to act as his "eyes and ears" during the intensive satellite commanding. And, he expects me to do the same.

I'm not sure I follow this logic as the contractor satellite engineers have it well in hand and are the experts. I'm no expert. Most of the contractors on site were in this business when I was still swinging from the monkey bars in third grade recess.

I feel in awe of some of these engineers; extremely talented and very smart. I'm not sure what value I can add to the daily commanding operations. But, I will gladly do it and I'm sure I'll learn a lot.

Eclipse Season Briefing
14 Feb 1990 Wednesday

At the morning meeting a discussion started about the upcoming eclipse season and the associated daily commanding. There seemed to be a lot of misconceptions about the process and eclipse season itself. The Aerojet contractor tried to explain but couldn't get his message across. His arcane, multiple acronyms, high tech, super detailed explanation was too complicated for most of the guys to follow. I looked around the room and saw eyes glossing over; faces looking frustrated; and folks starting to fidget. I was afraid that very shortly someone was going to yell out "STOP!"

I interjected.

"Sir, I think I can help. I can give an overview briefing to the crews about eclipse season. Just a top level brief on the eclipse phenomena, how it affects our satellite and the command procedure we'll use to mitigate the effects."

The DO took me up on the offer, "I want you to give that briefing tomorrow evening to all the crews members. I want everyone to attend including day staff. So, you guys will have to stay late."

Eclipse Brief Delivered

15 Feb 1990 Thurs

I got a nice feeling of accomplishment today. I feel like I'm part of the team.

I stayed after normal hours to give the crews a briefing on the upcoming eclipse season special commanding.

The conference room was packed as the DO made the briefing mandatory for all crew members. At first, I could sense a feeling in the room that collectively spoke to me, "Who is this new guy?"

The DO was there as well.

The briefing went well. I had a lot of confidence because I simply gave the same briefing we used to give the crews back in Denver. I started with a basic explanation of the eclipse season; when it starts, how long it lasts. I then talked about the eclipse phenomena and how it affects our satellite. Then I gave a general overview of the daily commanding procedure we'll use to lessen the effects of eclipse and keep our ability to detect launches at a high level.

The crews loved it. They'd never been told before. For them, eclipse season, was just a phrase; they didn't have a real sense of what was going on. And, technically they didn't have to as they can still do their job without this info. But, they really appreciated the insights because now they have a better understanding of what's happening around them and why it's happening.

After the briefing, a lot of crew members thanked me and gave me the positive feedback I just mentioned.

Printer Paper Delivery Service
16 Feb 1990 Friday

I made my first major change today. It was fairly easy and only time will tell if it all holds up. But, it should be fine as the change makes sense. The old way of doing the task didn't.

One of my duties – as pointed out to me by Sammy – is to check the contractor printer paper and make sure it's sufficiently stocked. Many satellite parameters are printed and then these printouts are stored. The printed data is saved so we can go back and look at it if required. Then it's thrown away after a certain period of time.

Well, my first question was, "Why am I doing this? Why is it my job to stock the paper? Don't we have a supply shop that does this kind of work for a living?"

It's not that I'm against doing such work; it's just that it doesn't make sense to me. What if I'm away, who stocks the paper then? Seems to me this task should be carried out by folks who already do this kind of work – like supply.

I figured the printer paper is something you always want to keep stocked; much the same as toilet paper. You run out of toilet paper at the wrong time and it all becomes a bit embarrassing. You run out of printer paper at the wrong time and you miss recording and storing a hardcopy printout of critical spacecraft parameters; another embarrassing situation.

I viewed the printout paper situation the same as the toilet paper situation. Why would you want to have only one person in charge of stocking toilet paper? What if that person is on holiday? Not good.

So, I started with the contractors. I noticed the printout paper stock was low so I went to supply and brought some to the contractor operations area. Then I started asking questions.

"Hey guys. How come Sammy stocked the printer paper? How come supply doesn't do it?"

Then the on-duty contractor satellite engineer, Don, piped up in a loud voice, "It's Sammy's job. He always made sure we had plenty of paper. We never ran out under Sammy's watch. The guy before Sammy was hopeless; but Sammy was the best. I hope you're gonna do as good a job as Sammy. Although them's some pretty big shoes to fill."

The other two contractors in the room shook their heads in agreement.

I ignored his comments and brought the focus back to my other question, "Yeah, but how come supply doesn't do it?"

"Supply can't do it! They're not allowed back here. They can't come into the contractor operations area. So, Sammy had to do it."

I was stunned by this answer; seemed so ridiculous. Yet, Don speaks with such authority; I generally believe what he tells me. I thought to myself, "Well, if that's the case then I'll do it. If supply can't come back here then that settles it; I'm stuck with the task and that's fine; I'm OK with it."

I said my polite goodbyes and walked out of the room dragging the hand trolley to deliver back to supply.

As I walked down the hallway I couldn't get out of my mind what Don said. "Supply can't do it!" You've got to be kidding. It just sounds wrong. It doesn't make sense. How can I just take this assertion on face value?

Then I came up with a dastardly idea. I'll do something crazy. I'll do something outside the norm of military thinking. I'll do something radical.

And so I did. I challenged Don's assertion. I felt a little guilty about it. After all, by doing so I was essentially calling Don a liar. I've been there before, when you question someone's assertion then they blurt out, "Are you calling me a liar?" In other words, you better just take what I say as gospel; you better not question me; you better just accept what I've told you as fact.

Well, I wasn't going to do that. Instead, I was going walk down to supply, return the trolley and then ask them to verify this ridiculous story I heard from Don.

"Hello Lt Mitchell. Thanks for bringing the trolley back," said Sgt Cahill in his usual big booming friendly way.

"Thanks for trusting me with it," I replied. Then I continued, "Sergeant Cahill, I want to ask you about stocking the printer paper for the contractors. Seems to me this task would be a nice fit for your work area. Is there any reason why you guys can't put this task in your job jar and take it over?"

"We tried to take it but Capt Jenks said he wanted to do it. He insisted on doing it."

I was taken aback by this response.

I continued, "So, there's nothing stopping you from checking the contractor printers from time to time and then restocking the paper when needed?"

"No sir."

"You have access to the contractor operations area; you guys can get in there ok; nothing stopping you?" I followed up because I couldn't believe what I was hearing.

"No problem. We go back there all the time. Our badge is cleared for that area. We can take over stocking the paper if you want us to," declared Sergeant Cahill.

And, that's how and when I turned the task over to the supply shop.

I have no idea what Don was talking about. And now I know Don doesn't either. Will I go back and ask Don for an explanation? Forget it.

I'm just thrilled to turn this task over to supply where it belongs. I got the result I was looking for; I'll leave it alone.

Somehow Don must have heard a story, believed it and stuck with it. And, now he tells it as if it's fact.

I'm so glad I questioned his story.

Lesson learned – verify, verify, verify!

Eclipse Commanding
21 Feb 1990 Wednesday

Starting several days ago, I've been going into work each night on the 7pm bus to support the eclipse commanding procedure. In the morning I attend the daily briefing, and then catch the bus home for some sleep.

Each night we send thousands of commands to the spacecraft to minimize the effects of the sun. During the eclipse season, the sun passes in front of the spacecraft barrel; not good for detecting missiles.

The commands go up rapid fire and so far the procedure has been working fine; no hiccups. It takes a little over two hours to complete the command sequence. The Aerojet engineer leads the procedure. The TRW engineer is watching to make sure the commanding doesn't interfere with other on-board subsystems. The Ground Station Operator (GSO) does all the keyboard entries; he starts the procedure to send all the commands via a command queue. Once he hits the "return" button, the commands start to fly.

My role as the DO's "eyes and ears" has been underwhelming other than I'm learning a lot about this special procedure and satellite commanding in general. The guys don't need me here, but they seem OK with having me around and they tolerate my questions and my sometimes over-curious nature. I guess they look at me as another guy suffering along with them during a mid-shift.

Aussie Accent

26 Feb 1990 Monday

Today I skirted a potentially embarrassing incident. At the same time, I discovered a serious weakness I need to overcome.

As a newcomer to Australia, I find myself having a difficult time understanding the Australian accent. And, this can cause embarrassment; as it almost did this morning at the daily briefing.

The briefing started at 8:30am sharp as usual. The DO gave his normal short brief and then each person at the table gives a short summary of what's happening in their section. When it came to my turn I put forward a request – on behalf of the contractors – for "tape time" so they could do some analysis. When I finished my explanation, the training department Chief, Capt Marcus, shot down my request, "Sorry Sean, all tape time is booked."

Capt Marcus is an interesting character. He's a sharp looking officer; clean cut; speaks with authority. He's not very tall, but he's built like a heavy lifting longshoreman. His military shirt puffs out around his waist because it's two or three sizes too big for his waist but just right for his shoulders, chest and arms. Finally, he seems to be very territorial and doesn't like to give up any resources, like tape training time. He almost had a twinkle in his eye as he informed me and everyone in the room that there is no training time available.

I thought that was the end of it until Capt Johnson spoke up. "Jono" is a highly respected crew commander and a member of the Australian Army. He launched into an animated discussion. His head moved back and forth. His hand gestures expressed a sincere willingness to get me the requested tape-time. His tone of voice suggested he had what I wanted.

But, there was an underlying problem. He didn't know it and no one else in the room knew it. But, I knew it. It was embarrassing.

The problem was this – I couldn't understand a word he said!

God knows I tried. I stared at him across the table as he spoke. I followed his lips to see if I could unravel the dialog that way. But, his lips were of no value – they hardly moved! That's Capt Johnson – almost no lip movement.

He finished his dialog with what sounded like a question. Then he handed the conversation back to me when he entered into a long pause.

It was during this pause that I could feel the beginnings of mild panic – embarrassment if you will – set in. Capt Johnson looked at me, waiting for my response. I stole a quick glance at the others in the room and they all seemed to have understood Capt Johnson's dialog and were now expectantly awaiting my response. I could also feel a slight tension in the room as everyone was looking for me to reply with the correct answer; an answer that Capt Johnson had spooned fed to me. He solved my problem, now all I had to do was acknowledge his gesture and agree to the proposal.

As I sat there my mind started racing, "What do I say? If I tell him "ok" and then he asks a follow up question, I'm dead! I've got to get out of this without ruining his offer to help. I've got to get out of this without admitting that I didn't understand a word he said!"

Then, in my flustered state, I formulated a response. I let out a hidden sigh of relief as I realized I may be able to escape this situation relatively unscathed. I would attempt to trick everyone into thinking I understood Capt Johnson's proposal and move the discussion smoothly to the next person at the table.

I decided it was my best option, so I put it to the test.

With all the confidence I could muster, I looked across the table and stated, *"Capt Johnson, that's an excellent idea. Let's get together after the meeting and discuss it further."*

My plan worked. The DO pointed to Capt Richmond sitting next to me and I was off the hot seat.

After the meeting, I shot up from my seat and dashed over to intercept Capt Johnson before he left the room.

"Capt Johnson, I'm really sorry but I have to admit something – I didn't understand a single word you said at the meeting."

His response was a classic. He let out a big roaring laugh and then told me, "Yeah, that's normal. A lot of the guys have trouble at first but don't you worry, we'll have you speaking correctly in no time!"

Capt Johnson went on to tell me he had reserved some tape time and he was willing to "donate" this tape time to the contractors.

Command Failure

18 Mar 1990 Sunday

Last night during our eclipse commanding we had a problem. The commands were going out as usual then all of the sudden ... they stopped. The command queue just sat there – not moving; frozen.

We'd never seen this before. The Aerojet engineer said, "Keep going. Restart the queue and let's get these commands out. If we don't we won't be set up in time for the eclipse."

The TRW engineer was more cautious, "Let's figure out what's going on. Let's figure out why the queue stopped."

After a few minutes, the TRW engineer reported his findings, "The last command didn't pass the functional verification check. The ground software didn't receive verification that the command went through."

Now the debate raged and I was in the middle.

"We need to get these commands out now. We can't wait. Mission will be degraded," the Aerojet engineer argued.

The TRW engineer asked for more time.

I asked the TRW engineer, "Hey George, how does the spacecraft look? Do you see anything wrong?"

"I don't see anything wrong. State of Health looks fine. I just want to understand why the ground software is not picking up the functional verification check," George replied.

"Well, do you feel it's OK to start up the queue again? Can we continue the commanding?" I asked.

"I think we'll be ok." George said reluctantly.

The Ground Station Operator (GSO) re-started the queue and all went fine ... for a while. Then the queue stopped again; same problem. No functional verification.

The TRW engineer went through his checks. All looked ok.

The crew commander, Aerojet engineer, TRW engineer, GSO and I had a quick pow-wow to discuss what to do.

"It's just going to keep doing this. For some reason, a few commands are not giving us any functional verification. But, we can see from telemetry that the threshold setting is what we commanded it to be. So, it appears the commands are getting through and it looks like it some kind of a ground station problem," explained George the TRW engineer.

He continued, "The only way we're going to get this queue finished is to bypass the ground station functional verification. If we set functional verification to "bypass" we'll get the commanding done. Otherwise, we'll miss the timeline and we'll have to call headquarters and tell them we'll have degraded mission."

The Aerojet engineer chimed in, "We better get moving or there's no reason to go on; we'll miss the window. I say we bypass functional verification and get the commands out."

"Everybody OK with bypassing functional verification?" I asked with a tinge of enthusiasm, looking for no dissension and no further discussion. After all, we isolated the problem to the ground station; no issues with the satellite.

We all agreed.

The GSO set functional verification to "bypass" and re-started the queue.

All commands went out successfully and in time for the eclipse. The mission sensors were configured per normal and mission was not negatively impacted.

We made it.

I felt pretty good about what we'd done. We had a problem. We assessed it. We made a decision based on the information available and with the possibility of mission degradation hanging over our head. And, then, finally, we executed the plan.

And, it looks like it was the correct decision as the commanding was successful.

Command Failure Fallout
20 Mar 1990 Tuesday

I just woke up from a deep sleep. The morning bus dropped me off in front of my flat at about 09:00 (9am). I barely remember walking through the door and collapsing on my bed. I think I was asleep before my body landed.

I haven't been home since Sunday evening when I took the 7pm bus into work.

Monday morning was not good for me. When the TRW day staff engineers got to work early Monday they started digging into our commanding problem from last Saturday night. They're screaming bloody murder. They can't believe we "bypassed" functional verification while commanding the satellite. They are in a tizzy about it.

And, because they're in a tizzy, so is the DO. He's not happy with me. I'm his "eyes and ears" and he thinks I let him down.

The DO thinks I'm a "cowboy." And, that's not a compliment. Right in front of the contractors and crew he let me have it, "Sammy wouldn't have authorized those commands. He would have shut it down. If we lose the satellite, we lose mission permanently. What would you rather have - mission down for two hours or mission down permanently?"

I'm in the doghouse.

* * *

So, instead of going home, I spent the day in meetings as the engineers searched for answers and a fix to the problem. At about 17:00 (5pm) local time I sent a message to headquarters explaining the commanding problem and the fix proposed by the contractor engineering team.

Here's what happened. For some reason the commands got out of sequence. The ground software was looking for the previous command sent but was seeing the next command sent. They didn't match, so the procedure shuts down. As long as the commands were out of sequence, we were never going to pass this ground functional verification check.

After working on it all day, the contractor engineers came up with a simple fix and we should no longer have this problem.

Last night we ran with the fix and had no problem. All commands went out with full functional verification; looks like we're out of the woods.

Too bad I'm not.

The DO thinks I played rough with the spacecraft. He thinks I leaned too far towards accomplishing the mission and not enough in safeguarding the spacecraft.

I don't agree. I feel pretty good about what we did; about carrying on with the commanding. After all, we were up against a time constraint. We had to make a decision – command and get optimum mission or stop commanding and degrade mission?

All indications suggested we had a ground problem, not a problem with the satellite. The satellite engineer felt it was OK to continue commanding while by-passing ground functional verification. With this information, I felt it best to proceed with the commanding. And, it turns out it was a ground problem and the satellite was not in danger. But, that's not how the day staff TRW engineers feel. And, it's not how the DO feels.

* * *

I finally got home this morning after spending over 36 hours at work! I collapsed. The first 24 hours of this long-long shift went by like a flash because I was running on adrenalin; I was working full on. I felt like I was trying to win my job back; like I was trying to convince the DO not to fire me.

But, yesterday when the day staff went home in the early evening – after we had a fix for the problem and things were under control – I started to fade. I could barely keep my eyes open last night during the eclipse commanding. Finally, after encouragement from the crew commander, the contractor engineers and the other crew members, I curled up under the GSO desk and dosed off.

The eclipse commanding went smoothly.

Command Failure Finale

22 Mar 1990 Thursday

The DO called a meeting this morning to hear all sides of the story; the story about what happened last Saturday night during the eclipse commanding procedure.

I was glad to hear we were having a meeting. I figured it would be a way to clear things up; maybe make the day staff folks stop their "Monday Morning Quarterbacking." But, at the same time I wasn't excited about attending. I just worked all night supporting the eclipse commanding procedure and I was tired; looking forward to going home to sleep. But, sleep would have to wait.

The Aeroject engineers were backing the decision to continue commanding; they were 100% in favor. No surprise since they're the mission guys and their main focus is on mission.

Surprisingly, the TRW guys were also generally supportive saying we were in a tight spot; a time critical spot and the satellite appeared to be in no danger. Ideally, they'd prefer a more cautious approach which would mean suspending all commanding until we understand the problem completely. But, they concede, based on the information available and the mission requirements, the on-duty crew did the right thing by continuing the command sequence and configuring the satellite to optimize for best mission capability.

Finally, the DO conceded he would probably have made the same decision.

"Based on all the evidence, I probably would have given the go-ahead to continue commanding. It's a grey area and there's risk involved but sometimes you gotta go with the limited information available and you gotta go with your gut.

"But, if the satellite all of the sudden went into a backward graceful tumble because we sent an erroneous command, I wouldn't want to have to explain it to headquarters. From now on, I'd like to err on the side of caution. If we don't fully understand a commanding problem, I want all commanding to stop until we do.

"We got out of this one OK and I guess we should just count ourselves lucky."

It was a backhanded concession. Yes, he would have done the same thing we did, but don't do it again.

Seems like the message here is – cover your ass; cover your career; don't make any mistakes; don't make any decisions that involve risk; make the safe bet.

I don't like this style of play.

"You're a Cowboy"

24 Mar 1990 Saturday

I was hanging out with Capt Rob Frentani this afternoon and found out his feelings about my role in the satellite commanding fiasco from last weekend.

Rob is an Air Force Academy grad. He's a crew commander; good officer; smart guy; conscientious; we get along pretty well.

Rob has a stocky build, jet black hair, a square jaw and a serious outlook on life. To me he looks like he should be starring in the next Rocky movie; he looks like your classic prizefighter.

He was visiting at my flat and surprised me when he stated, "You're a cowboy Sean. We don't need cowboys in ops. You did the wrong thing by continuing with the commanding last weekend. The DO called you a cowboy."

I was taken aback. What's he talking about? He wasn't there. How does he know what happened? He's making a judgment without even finding out my side of the story.

I paused to gather my thoughts.

"Rob, what are you talking about?" I figured that would put him on the defensive. I wanted him to justify his comments.

"You could have sent a bad command. You were commanding blind. You should have stopped the commanding. What authority did you have to continue commanding? The safety of the spacecraft comes first. If I was the crew commander on duty, I would have stopped it. I would rather take the mission hit than risk the safety of the satellite."

I couldn't believe what I was hearing. It sounded so text book; so "Monday morning quarterback"; so condescending; so preaching.

He talked like the guy who looked up the answer in the back of the book then brags about how he got it right.

To me, Rob is just going along with the DO's perspective. The DO thinks I should have stopped the commanding and taken the mission hit, so that's the line Rob's going with. That's what it sounds like to me.

"Rob, my TRW guy said the spacecraft was fine. We checked telemetry and it said the commands sent had taken correctly. The only error we were getting was the ground software saying there's no functional verification. Everything else looked good. We isolated it to a ground problem. Now, we had to make a decision. Are we going to take a mission hit for a ground problem? I didn't feel we should do that and the other engineers and crew commander agreed. I think we did the right thing," I stated in a low, measured and slightly irritated voice.

"You were taking a big risk. It worked out OK but that's what I mean by 'cowboy.' You take unnecessary risks. And, that's not how ops works. You safeguard the satellite first; the satellite safety and health always comes first," Rob continued his sermon.

I couldn't believe my ears. Why is Rob driving this home so hard? Why is he so concerned about this incident? It's been sorted. I felt it was behind us; behind me. But, he was throwing it up in my face again as if he wanted me to repent, or start crying or resign from the Air Force.

This episode has really tainted my impression of Rob. From now on, I'll be careful what I do and say around him. He seems too much like the kind of guy that lets the boss do his critical thinking for him. He seems like he just looks to the boss and says, "Tell me what to think." If the DO says Sean is a cowboy, then Sean is a cowboy. No need to gather any facts, the DO has spoken. No need to ask Sean what happened, the DO has told me what to think.

I don't respect this kind of thinking. I don't like it.

Military Ball: OK to Go

10 Apr 1990 Tuesday

I'm very excited. The DO gave me the OK to attend a military ball this weekend in Adelaide. This will be the first time I've left town since I arrived. And, it will be the first day off I've had in over a seven weeks. I've been going in every single night – even weekends – to support the eclipse commanding.

I've kind of been hoping the DO would offer to let me have a night off now and again, but he hasn't made any such offers. And, I haven't been game to ask. He carries on as if it's normal for me to work every day – no days off. When I think about asking him for a night off, I remember his words, "Sammy worked every day during eclipse season. And, I expect you to do the same."

The other officers have been asking me to go to the ball. It's at the RAAF Base Edinburgh north of Adelaide and it's over the upcoming Easter holiday weekend. We get both the Friday and Monday off; a long four day weekend. The Friday holiday is Good Friday and then there's Easter Monday. I suppose the Monday holiday is to recover from all the Easter Sunday celebrating.

I told them eclipse season isn't over and I've got to go in to support the commanding. But, they encouraged me to ask the DO for the time off. So I did.

Today I got up the courage, "Sir, there's a military ball coming up over this long holiday weekend. I was wondering if it would be alright for me to get some time off to go?"

I was all set to launch into a long winded explanation of how the eclipse season is almost over; the commanding procedure is very well understood; we haven't had any issues; but I didn't have to.

When I went to get a gulp of air, the DO interjected, "Yeah, go ahead Sean. You've been working hard, you deserve a break."

I was stunned. I was also smart enough to end the conversation quickly saying, "Ok sir." And, I walked away – quickly.

Military Ball – Wrap Up

16 Apr 1990 Monday

I just got back from Adelaide. I attended the military ball at the RAAF Base Edinburgh officers club. The base is located about 25 km north of the city.

This is my first time off work for what seems like an eternity. I think I worked over 40 days straight! Anyway, I lost count.

What a relief it was to leave the village and make the road trip south. It was great to get in my car and drive down the track. I shipped my little Toyota Corolla over from Colorado. It's a "left hand drive" which makes it a bit difficult when driving over here in Australia. The Aussies drive on the left side of the road with the steering wheel on the right side of the car. But, I've made the adjustment and driving my "left hand" vehicle is not a problem.

I loaded up my car with three other officers and we headed down the track. The first 169 km was essentially straight road and lots of desert. Then we hit the small town of Port Augusta where we stopped and loaded up on junk food – Hungry Jacks! Hungry Jacks is the same as Burger King. Not sure why it's got a different name.

Then another three hours to Adelaide and the RAAF (Royal Australian Air Force) Base. We stayed in the barracks; we got there on Friday evening.

Saturday morning we ducked down to the city for a bit of time by the beach. We lounged in the sun and sand at Glenelg, right at the end of the tram line in Adelaide.

I almost had to pinch myself as I stared in amazement at all the sights. I was beginning to think I had floated off to heaven as I contemplated the incredible scene; sandy beach, ocean waves, beautiful bikini girls, the smell of gourmet coffee and fresh bread baking.

After our day at the beach we headed back north to the barracks and got dressed up in our formal military uniforms and then walked over to the officer's club.

The event started with drinks in the lobby. I engaged an Australian officer in conversation. Somehow we got onto the subject of ANZAC

Day. He became very emotional as he described how much it means to Australians. He talked about how the soldiers struggled for months on the beach head at Gallipoli; how they got slaughtered; how they were left to fend for themselves. I was interested and listening intently until he finally cut off our talk by saying, "You wouldn't understand." He then walked away. The word that comes to mind is ... awkward.

But, I did appreciate his insights on ANZAC Day and what it means to Australians. I plan to research this event more and find out what makes it such a special holiday.

I enjoyed the military ball but it followed more or less the usual formula. Start off with a few toasts – one of them to the Queen; then followed by a few short speeches; then the meal and finally dancing and socializing.

Sunday morning and the car loaded with four slightly hung over Woomera guys, the Corolla headed back north to our Australian outback home.

It was great to escape work and Woomera even for only a few days.

ANZAC Day Article; Gibber Gabber

18 Apr 1990 Wed

My curiosity about ANZAC day got the better of me so on Tuesday I did some research and started taking notes. After rereading my notes and making a few adjustments I found the makings of a decent article. I figured others may find it interesting and informative.

ANZAC Day is a major Australian holiday so I figured it might be a good idea to find out more about it. The day marks the landing of the Australian and New Zealand Army Corp (ANZAC) at Gallipoli on 25 April 1915. It's a long and sad story about how the ANZACs took a beating by the Turks for about eight months before finally getting evacuated to safety. How anyone could live on that beachhead for eight months is beyond me. Many ANZACs didn't.

Anyway, I took my completed article over to the Gibber Gabber office and offered it for publication. The Gibber is our local village paper. It normally contains village announcements; I figured they'd tell me to get lost.

But, I was somewhat surprised when the lady accepted my article and told me, "We'll look at it and see if it's a good fit for the paper."

Regardless, I felt good about doing the research and putting the article together and then offering to the Gibber as a way of sharing what I discovered with others in the village who may not know about the origin of ANZAC Day. I'll bet most of the Yanks have no idea.

Gibber Article Feedback
23 Apr 1990 Monday

I was surprised to pick up a copy of the Gibber Gabber on Friday to discover my article was headline news! It was featured on the front page.

I was also surprised by the feedback. Most people were very positive, thanking me for sharing my research. They generally had no idea about the origin of ANZAC Day.

I have a real sense of satisfaction about the article. It was enjoyable to research, to write and then to see it published in the village paper. Finally, it was rewarding to get such uplifting and positive feedback. Although one Aussie lady had a backhanded "go" at me, "Nice article Sean, what book did you steal it from?"

ANZAC Day is this Wednesday. We have the day off. There will be a dawn service and then we head to the RSL (Returned Serviceman's League) Club for breakfast and other activities. I'm looking forward to it.

ANZAC Day
25 Apr 1990 Wednesday

I attended the ANZAC Day celebration today. It started with an early morning dawn ceremony commemorating the Gallipoli landings on this day back in 1915. Then we all headed off to "breakie" (as the Aussies call breakfast) at the RSL Club.

It wasn't too long before I noticed the beer caps coming off and the bottles turning upwards and the beer flowing downwards. Then I noticed a bit of commotion and saw a group of people circled around a guy tossing coins in the air. The game is called "Two up" and apparently this gambling game is only legal on ANZAC Day. From what I saw, the Aussies love this game. Whooping and yelling all around.

PART 2: MAY – JUL 1990

Lt Kelly Gets Decertified

4 May 1990 Friday

Australian Navy Lieutenant Ethan Kelly came by my office today. He was very upset. He wanted to get something off his chest. I was glad to listen.

"Sean, I got decertified yesterday. I'm back in today for retraining. What a joke!"

He was taking a short break from his retraining and popped into my office to let off some steam.

Lt Kelly is one of the best Crew Commander's on site. He stands about 6 feet tall with blonde hair that's almost white. He's 28 years old and has been at site longer than any other crew commander. He exudes confidence.

As a Navy Lieutenant, his rank is the equivalent of an Army Captain.

Lt Kelly has a reputation for "knowing his stuff" and the troops think he's the greatest. He seems to have a natural grasp on the art of leadership. He knows when to be tough; when to lighten up. And, the troops respond with loyalty and admiration; they do what he says and they do it willingly.

He's in training today to get re-certified. Once re-certified he can go back to crew. All the training guys know it's a joke because Lt Kelly can run circles around them on the ops floor; he knows more about the position than they do.

But, them's the rules and he's got to go through the re-certification process like everyone else; military inefficiency at work.

"How can I be decertified for getting it right?" He asked rhetorically.

"What are you talking about?" I replied. Even though my office is right next to the ops floor and I work closely and interact with the crews a lot, I still don't know the inside information unless the guys tell me.

I think that's one of the reasons the crews like talking to me about their troubles – I am an outsider; I have no stake in the crew game.

"Do you know why they decertified me? Because I sent the launch 'high speed.' It was a missile launch and I sent it high speed. Isn't that what we're here to do? I did the right thing – made the right call – and they decertified me anyway. Tell me, how does that work?" He blurted out.

"I don't get it. Why would they de-cert you for that?" I questioned.

"It was just an SRBM (short range ballistic missile) and it didn't meet all the criteria for a high speed send. But, I knew it was a launch – coming out of a known area, at the right time – we've seen them before, we all know it's a launch. I'd feel guilty sending it low speed when I know it's a real launch. Yes, I was taking a risk but it was a calculated risk based on lots of experience. I knew I was right – I sent it. And, we found out shortly after wards – it was confirmed as a valid launch. So, I was right. Doesn't matter – the WING sent a message telling the DO to follow procedures and decertify me. The DO tried to stick up for me but the WING wouldn't budge – decertify him and put him through retraining they said. You don't send high speed – EVER – unless all launch criteria is met; period; no discussion."

I couldn't believe what I was hearing. I knew the military was quirky, but this was taking it over the cliff. Let me get this straight, the guys lets you know a missile has been launched and you punish him for it. The guy has done his job – to an outstanding level; taken a calculated risk; got it right – and you punish him for it? And, this makes sense?

Lt Kelly continued, "This is going to cause big problems for you guys. Us Aussies can get away with it, our careers aren't ruined because of some stupid headquarters decision. I just have to explain the whole thing to the Wing Commander, he'll talk to my Navy bosses and it's all good. When they explain what I've done they'll have a good laugh and say, Bloody Dumb Yanks!"

He kept going and I was more than willing to listen to his down home spun Aussie common sense.

"But, you guys will be in trouble. Nobody is going to send anything high speed unless it meets every one of their stupid criteria. That means valid launches are going to get missed; they'll go out of here 'low speed.' And, according to headquarters you can never be wrong sending out something low speed. It may be a bit embarrassing sending a big blooming – light up the whole screen – ICBM out low speed, but they won't decertify you for it. They'd be upset but they couldn't decertify you for it.

"And, that's the kind of environment they're creating; one where nobody wants to make a mistake; where everyone is protecting their career. So, instead of doing the job well, we'll all be looking to save our necks – especially you YANKs - one mistake and it becomes a career ending black mark on your record. It's crazy. I don't know how you guys run a military like this!"

I wasn't exactly excited to hear this negative commentary on the US military, but I couldn't find the fault in his logic; seemed to me like I was hearing the ugly, unfiltered, unadulterated truth.

Just then Captain Marcus came through the door to let Lieutenant Kelly know it was time to go back to training.

Lieutenant Kelly rolled his eyes, got up slowly from the chair and said, "See ya Sean, gotta help Capt Marcus figure out how to set up the training tapes."

Dance with Navy Girl
6 May 1990 Sunday

Being a single officer in town can be a bit awkward sometimes; especially, when it comes to socializing with the single enlisted ladies. There are a few enlisted gals in town who are – shall we say – nicely put together. And, they can be very friendly and I wouldn't mind getting to know them better – a lot better.

Technically, the female enlisted gals are off limits to officers. We even had a briefing recently where the DO – Lt Col French – gathered us all into a room and delivered his best General Patton imitation speech about the f-word – fraternization.

"It's come to my attention that some enlisted and officers are developing unprofessional relationships. I've heard enlisted personnel call officers by their first name ... doesn't matter if you're out of uniform – you don't do it. And, officers, don't let the enlisted folks get away with it. I'm told officers are dating enlisted personnel. This has to stop. We can't run a professional unit if discipline breaks down. You must realize, the officer's career is in jeopardy for breaking fraternization rules. If you respect your officers, don't fraternize."

Lt Col French was trying to come down like a "bad-ass" but it wasn't working. His personality isn't really suited for being the bad guy. But, everyone respects him enough to want to follow his direction. I certainly do.

It seems to me there are some things you just can't order around – like human nature. I think human nature will trump Lt Col

French's fraternization rules every time. His speech – especially the part dealing with dating between enlisted and officer – seems to fly in the face of reality. And, as such, comes off to me as a bit comical.

Ordering men and women to not date is like ordering rain to fall upwards. You can pass the order but it won't have any effect; the rain is gonna fall downwards and the dating will continue.

Also, these days there are more and more cases of officers marrying enlisted personnel. It happens a lot. How does that happen without dating? It doesn't.

So, to say officers can't date enlisted appears silly when you see officers married to enlisted members. They obviously dated; they're still in the service; no careers are in jeopardy. Nah, the 'no dating' order just doesn't add up; doesn't make sense.

Also, if dating is considered fraternization then what's it called when an officer and enlisted person are married? Is there a classification higher than fraternization? Couldn't it be argued that marriage goes above and beyond – way beyond – fraternization? Wouldn't you say, if two people are married, they've gone way past fraternization?

So, let me get this straight, you're going to kick out an officer for dating an enlisted person, but everything's alright if they're married? How does that make sense?

It doesn't. And, that's why people don't follow it. That's why people ignore it. Besides, let's get down to the nitty-gritty here – the bottom line – the reality of the situation ...

YANKS IN THE OUTBACK

How are you going to stop it? How are you going to stop men and women from getting together? How are you going to stop human nature?

And, now for the drum roll ...

Why would you even try?

What a waste of energy and resources. You're going to kick people out for being human; for carrying on with basic human behavior; behavior that's always going to trump your rules and regulations.

Ordering males and females to stop dating each other is like ordering the troops to stop eating. Are people going to stop eating just because you gave the order? You'd have a hard time carrying out that order. It would be a waste time. People must eat to live.

Similarly, people seek partners to marry and have families. That's what people do.

Good luck trying to stop it.

* * *

Well, Lt Col French's speech was going through my mind as I stood at the disco last night glancing at several of the beautiful looking enlisted ladies. And, shall I add – friendly; nice to talk to; nice to dance with; nice to spend time with.

I was putting on my best behavior face and steering clear of the enlisted ladies. I was trying to follow the guidance from the brass.

So, I sat down at a table with some of the married civilian ladies and single ladies who work at the shops in town. Not a bad place to hang out because these ladies are also good looking, dressed nicely and friendly as well.

I was enjoying the dancing and then the music went to a slow song. I left the dance floor and stood up watching the other couples pair up and start slow dancing.

I glanced over across the room. I could almost feel the presence of someone looking at me. And, then I saw her; a young, very nicely dressed, good looking lady. She's about as tall as me, with blonde brown hair, creamy skin – a real cutie. And, wouldn't you know, she's in the US Navy; enlisted.

I looked at her and gave her a big smile. That's when she started walking over to me. She came right up near my face and said, "Lt Mitchell, would you like to dance."

What could I say?

Here are a few responses I ruled out immediately.

- *Ah- no thanks. You remember the speech Lt Col French gave recently about fraternization ... blah, blah, blah.*
- *Oh, I'd love to but I hurt my big toe on the last dance.*
- *Sorry, but I've got to go home right now; I have some regulations I need to read up on.*

Instead, I responded as follows:

"Sure!"

As we danced I felt guilty. Not because we were dancing; not because she was enlisted; but, because I didn't ask her to dance first!

I thoroughly enjoyed our dance. It was very nice to put my arms around an attractive gal with our bodies gently colliding from time to time. I didn't mind the collisions and I probably caused a few on purpose.

Following the dance I escorted her off the dance floor and she went back with her group of friends. I went back to my table.

I'm not sure Lt Col French would approve of my dance floor antics. But, I have a sneaking suspicion he wouldn't really care. He was a young single guy once. And, I'd have to ask him, "What would you have done if you were in my shoes?"

All seems a bit silly. And, I'll bet I'm not the only one thinking it. And, I'll bet Lt Col French feels that way too but he has to tow the party line. He has to make it look like he's upholding the "rain must fall upwards" order.

First Aid Response Team
10 May 1990 Thursday

We have a new site nurse. She's not new to the site but she just started in her new position this week and she's off to a blazing start. She got everyone's attention but it caused her a bit of embarrassment.

I really appreciate what she did because it gave everyone a good laugh and she seems to be taking the whole thing in stride. Good sport.

Angela used to work in the cafeteria serving and preparing meals; the next thing you know she's appointed as our new site nurse.

Welcome to Woomera … these things happen here.

She wasn't the friendliest lady on the cafeteria staff but she was one of the youngest and also one of the prettiest. She came across as gruff and unhappy during the times I interacted with her. I would usually avoid her and just talk with the older lunch ladies who are much friendlier.

But, I noticed a change in Angela this week. She's very upbeat and excited about her new position as the site nurse. She was telling me her ideas and although I don't remember much about the details, I remember her enthusiasm. I wasn't listening very closely to what she was saying, I was distracted by the fact that she was even talking to me and that she was so positive and upbeat. I thought, "Is this the same Angela? She's not herself and it's a big improvement!"

Angela's first official act as the new site nurse really caused a stir.

* * *

It all started on Tuesday when she sent out a site wide memo describing her new initiative. She's forming a "First Aid Response Team."

Her memo was very well written and I could feel her enthusiasm jump out at me. It was contagious. After reading the memo I wanted to join the new team.

But, I wondered if she read it closely before sending it out. I wondered if she thought to have someone else read it first before sending it out to the entire site. I wondered if anyone else would notice what I noticed.

The next day, Wednesday, I got my answer. Someone did notice and just to let everyone know, sent out a reply memo.

The reply memo was very formal and came from TSgt Sims from "Commo" (Communications section). I knew it was going to be a must read because we hardly ever see memos from Commo and never from TSgt Sims. He didn't disappoint. You could tell he put a lot of effort into this one. I wonder if he puts this much effort into doing his real work?

He set the tone right upfront in the Subject line ...

    SUBJ: First Aid Response Team (FART)

Then he started to grind ...

> *I would like to congratulate you on the formation of the First Aid Response Team (FART). I can hardly believe we've gone this long without a FART. It seems to me a FART is critical to site operations. Without a FART we cannot be expected to operate at optimum level. Just knowing a FART is on-site ready to appear at a moment's notice is reassuring.*

And, on and on it went!

I saw Angela later that day (Wed) and I was glad to see her in good spirits. She was laughing as hard as the rest of us. She quickly told me she changed the name of the "TEAM" – to what I don't remember. Nothing can be as catchy as her original!

I was relieved to see Angela enjoying her "mistake" as much as everyone else and now she's moving on. That way I didn't have to feel so guilty about how much I enjoyed reading TSgt Sims' reply memo.

DO is Leaving
14 May 1990 Monday

Found out today that Lt Col French's replacement will be arriving in late June. We're told he's a Major but will pin on Lt Colonel sometime after he arrives.

Smoking Area Incident

17 May 1990 Thursday

I went somewhere today that I've never been before. A place reserved for special people. I am not a special person and the folks in the "special" area let me know it.

What is this special place?

None other than the designated smoking area!

Why did I go there?

Glad you asked.

I was having a conversation with SSgt Myers about some technical issue – I forget what it was – and he interrupted the conversation and said he had to go outside for a smoke.

I was going to suggest we meet in 15 minutes and then on further consideration I thought, "Hey, why don't I just go with him to the smoking area and talk with him there?"

I thought it was a good idea. But, I don't think SSgt Myers thought much of it. He looked at me a bit strange as I walked by his side down the hallway on our way to the smoking area.

I continued our conversation, asking questions, explaining my situation and he looked at me as if to say, "You do realize I'm going to the smoking area, right?"

He started to lighten up a bit as he responded to my questions and we continued our walk. If I had to hazard a guess as to what he was thinking, I'd suggest, "Hey maybe Lt Mitchell is a smoker. We'll have a cigarette together."

SSgt Myers pushed open the door to the smoking area and the two of us entered the scene. The smoking area is simply a concrete ramp on the side entrance of the building. It's not very big and there's a railing so people can lean on it and look cool as they smoke. I'd say there were at least 10 people out there smoking.

As I walked onto the concrete ramp all was fine until I stopped next to SSgt Myers – who proceeded to light up a cigarette – and continued our conversation.

It didn't take long for me to notice I was the only person talking in the smoking area. Everyone else went silent. Then I noticed SSgt Myers attention drifting as he could sense the mood change and the penetrating stares from his fellow smokers.

Smokers know who the smokers are; they know I'm not a smoker. Their silence was so loud, I could almost hear them shouting, "Why is this non-smoker invading our space? What's he doing out here? He doesn't belong."

I started thinking fast. What do I say? Is there anything I can do to diffuse this tense moment; this pregnant silence?

Then, I went into acting mode. I decided to have a bit of fun with this silly situation.

"Excuse me! Excuse me everyone!" I called out to get their attention as I waived my hands out wide like a circus show announcer.

The mood became even more intense as I felt the collective response of my smoking audience. They seemed to be saying, "Oh my God, now the non-smoker is going to talk! He's going to tell us the hazards of smoking. He's going to give us a lecture on lung cancer. Get him out of here – NOW!"

Then very slowly and deliberately I asked my silent and stunned audience a simple question ...

"Does anyone here mind if I .... DON'T SMOKE?"

It worked. They all started laughing and I was accepted as an honorary smoker.

I continued my conversation with SSgt Myers and the other smokers went back to their animated conversations.

HQ Data Request

18 May 1990 Friday

Headquarters (HQ) made a request today. They want data. One of the boxes on-board the satellite is acting up and our local site contractor engineers have been investigating it. They've been reporting their findings but HQ is not satisfied. HQ doesn't believe the results or just thinks our site guys aren't smart enough to figure it out.

What HQ doesn't seem to understand is we don't work in isolation. Our local site Aerojet engineers are in constant contact with the Aerojet experts back at the plant in Azusa, California. They are analyzing the data as well. We've got the best people working on it.

Still not good enough for HQ. They want us to send them data so they can do independent analysis.

The lead Aerojet engineer Karl Henry took this data request as an action item. I happened to bump into Karl today and saw him standing by the printer as it threw off reams and reams of paper.

"What are you doing Karl?" I asked noticing he seemed to be having altogether way too much fun standing by the printer with a smirk on his face.

"Headquarters wants data? I'll give em data. I'll give them enough data to keep them busy for the next year. I'm gonna dump the whole load on em," he said in an almost maniacal tone.

"What are they going to do with the data?" I asked.

Karl answered as if he was really glad I asked, "Nothing. They'll do absolutely nothing with it. There's nobody there who knows anything about this subsystem. They just want to make it look like they're doing something. They want to show us who's in charge. They call for data; we have to deliver. So, we'll deliver. Once I send them all this, they'll never ask for data again!"

The stack of paper was already almost a foot tall. I think he stopped printing when the paper stack reached two feet.

I had a good laugh. Headquarters is not a popular word at site. We look at them as busy bodies. Every time they get tasked to do something, they simply pass the task onto us. We have nobody else below us, so we end up doing it. Normally these HQ tasks are meaningless, time wasting exercises. A typical HQ task would be something like this ...

Some HQ staffer goes to a meeting in Colorado. At the meeting some general wonders if the Australian crew commanders are better – make fewer mistakes - than the US crew commanders. The next thing you know we get official tasking from HQ to come up with metrics showing personnel errors with a focus on the nationality of the offender. So, we drop everything and start putting together a report. While we're in the process HQ is calling every day to find out when it's going to be completed.

HQ wants it faster so they send a formal message giving us a deadline. The usual deadline is COB (close of business) tomorrow – one day.

Somehow our guys manage to meet the deadline and our DO avoids getting a nasty phone call from HQ.

Then we find out the truth.

The DO asks at the morning meeting, "Hey have you heard anything back from HQ on the report we sent? Have they got back with any word from the General?"

No one's heard a thing.

"Well, I want you to call HQ and ask them for some feedback on the report. Our guys put the work in; worked extra hours to get it done; I want some feedback." The DO commands.

The next morning at the meeting the feedback is in.

"Well, what did they say?" The DO asks.

"Sir, HQ hasn't even looked at it. It turns out something more important has come up and they are too busy. Chances are they'll never look at it."

"You mean to tell me we pulled guys off other tasks to get this report for some general and then they're not even going to look at it; they're not going to use it?"

"Yes, sir."

Is it any wonder Karl was having so much fun printing off a stack of data for HQ? Karl knows it's a waste of time. He also knows he's got to do it. So, why not have a bit of fun while complying with another dumb, time wasting, HQ request?

Mud Stomping Incident

21 May 1990 Monday

I just got into my office this morning when the phone rang. It was the DO - Lt Col French - and he had a very unusual question for me.

YANKS IN THE OUTBACK

"Hey Sean, did you come in the front door this morning stomping your feet and getting mud all over the front hallway?"

I thought about it for a moment before the vision came back to me. I remembered having mud caked all over my combat boots and how it wouldn't come off. I remember stomping my feet but I thought I only did it on the matting surface at the door entrance. But, as I thought more I recalled continuing to stomp past the matting surface. There were a lot of people behind me trying to get in so it seemed a bit awkward to block them by standing stationary and stomping on the mat, so I kept moving and kept stomping. The area in front of the mat was already dirty so I figured I'd just continue getting the mud off so I didn't track it all the way through the building; keep the mess in the general area of the front door.

"Yes, sir, I was stomping my feet to get the mud off so I wouldn't bring it all the way into the building." I finally answered.

"Well, great job. You better get to the front door right now and apologize to the cleaning lady before we have an international incident on our hands!" He blurted in a style commensurate with an angry Lt Colonel.

I took off down the hallway to the front entrance.

There she was, the cleaning lady – Fiona – mopping up all the mud. She was not happy. She had a scowl on her face. I approached with caution.

Fiona is in her twenties, blonde hair, soft spoken; a pretty gal.

"Hello Fiona, I just want to say I'm very sorry for coming in here this morning and stomping my boots all over your nice clean floor," I groveled.

I winced and closed my eyes waiting for the mop to strike me across the head.

Instead I heard Fiona's sweet voice, "It's ok. You weren't the only one. Almost everyone was doing it. I just got done mopping the floor; it was spotless and then the morning rush came in and trashed it. I was pissed but I'm over it now."

"Can I help you clean up?" I groveled some more.

"Noy, I got it. I'm almost done. Just next time wipe your feet only on the mat don't keep stomping and wiping on the clean floor, ok?" She asked rhetorically in her kickin Aussie accent.

I left the scene in one piece. I survived. I averted an international incident.

New Satellite Coming

22 May 1990 Tuesday

I just got official confirmation today that we'll be getting a second satellite sometime in November or December this year. The DO assigned me to head up the Ground Station Readiness (GSR) team to make sure we're set to receive the new satellite.

I've never done anything like this before. It's going to be a challenge but we've got a lot of good people here who have been through this before. I will be relying on their expertise.

Phony Australian Accents
29 May 1990 Tuesday

I'm amazed at the Australian accent; or any accent for that matter. I guess I'm just lost in my own world where I think everyone should speak the way I do. I have this crazy idea that anyone who speaks with a different accent must be somehow faking it – you can't really talk that way for real?

I remember hearing the heavy Texas accent down in San Antonio at basic military training. We were cleaning up the dormitory. I asked my fellow recruit – who happened to be from Texas – "Have you mopped the hallway floor?" And, he looked at me with a straight face and in a molasses thick Texas accent said –

"I done did it."

I responded to him in a very uncreative way – I gave him my best blank stare. I couldn't believe what I just heard. I couldn't believe someone would answer me that way and be serious. I stood there waiting for him to burst out laughing and tell me he was just kidding around; he really didn't talk that way; he just wanted to get a reaction out of me. But, as I stood there, my jaw firmly resting on the ground, the laughter never came – he was serious. He "DONE DID" finished mopping the hallway floor! And, he looked at me as if to say, "Can't you understand plain English?"

The crazy part about this whole episode is I now find myself using that very phrase and I'm also not afraid to kick in a good Yankee attempt at the Texas accent! I love saying it. It reminds me of my basic training buddy from Texas and the big shock I got from his fabulous Texas attitude, phrasing and accent. I can understand why people easily fall into the down home Texas and/or southern USA accent. It's homey, it's comfortable, and it's friendly.

Well, today I ran into some more accent drama – or in my case – trauma! I'm fascinated by the Australian accent because it appears to be an accent you must work at; not one you fall into like the southern accent. And, yet there's one common denominator – the Australians have the accent down pat! They don't struggle with it at all. They roll with it; they live in it; they're the best at it; they've got it down! And, it sounds great.

My trauma came in the cafeteria. I entered to get my usual nice hot cup of coffee. But, for some reason, I detoured through the empty chow line to inspect the food on offer for lunch. It was then that I got into a conversation with the lunch ladies.

"Hi Betsy, what's on the menu today?" I asked.

"Sean, you got eyes, read what's on the board. Or, if you're really clever just look through the glass and see for yourself," came Betsy's cutting but fun loving reply. Betsy's been working in the kitchen for years and she's a tough Aussie who doesn't put up with any nonsense – especially from some young whippersnapper Yank asking stupid questions!

It was at this moment that I starting getting up the courage to have a bit of fun with Betsy. I feel comfortable with her. I thought I could get away it. Yes, I decided to have a go at her in a nice way; hopefully she'd take it that way and all would be fine.

So, I walked to the end of food serving line; right in front of the cash registers. I then signaled Betsy to come over in a way that says, "I have a secret to tell you."

Then, with Betsy behind one of the cash registers, I leaned forward slightly, cupped my hand over my mouth so only she could see my lips and I whispered loudly,

"Betsy, I've been in town for a while now so you can knock off the phony Australian accent."

Betsy looked at me with dismay. She yelled out with her thick, authentic, true blue Aussie accent, "Hey, Margaret - Come here. Sean says we can knock off our phony Australian accents! Can you believe he said that?"

Margaret came running over and jumped into the fray, "Phony Australian accents? What about your phony bloody American accent. Worst accent I've ever heard. When are you going to start speaking normal like us?"

I started laughing and they started laughing. I laughed with my foreign American accent; they laughed like true Aussies!

I finally got my coffee and left the cafeteria – surprisingly unhurt!

Sammy's Girlfriend

2 Jun 1990 Saturday

I went to the disco last night and had a lot more fun than I imagined. It was held at the ELDO which is a hotel, restaurant and nightclub near the center of the village. ELDO stands for European Launch Development Organization and harks back to the days when the British were here launching rockets.

The disco last night was much more fun than going to nightclubs back in Denver. The main reason for this is simple. When I walked into the disco last evening by myself, I was greeted by many smiling faces and shouts of "Hey! About time you got here! I've been looking for a dance partner! Hey, I got the first dance with Lt Mitchell!"

I felt like I was attending a family reunion – one where everyone gets along and everyone likes each other! I was taken aback by the welcoming and friendly atmosphere; I'm still trying to get used to it.

Sammy's girlfriend Jill was there last night and I had a few dances with her. She's a cutie but she's still head-over-heels for Sammy. That's fine. She asked me if I'd heard from Sammy. I said no. I don't really expect to hear from him as he's off on an ROTC instructor assignment somewhere in Florida. Then I fell for the bait and asked her, "How bout you - Have you heard from Sammy?"

I shouldn't have asked. She just about broke down in tears as she told me she hadn't heard a thing – nothing.

They Call Me "Bluey"
4 Jun 1990 Monday

As I sat in at my desk this morning I heard someone calling out, "Hey, Lt Mitchell, how do you like your new door sign?"

I walked through the open door from my office to the ops floor and there was Lt Lowe smiling and pointing up at the sign over my door. It was one word – "Bluey."

Lt Lowe is about my age and has been stationed with the RAAF in Darwin, Katherine and now Woomera. He's a likeable guy; a good officer.

"Bluey – what's that?" I asked.

"That's your name. That's the name we give to anybody with red hair. So, you're Bluey," Lt Lowe explained with a big smile and with enough volume for folks in Port Augusta to hear.

I'm not sure I like my new name but I knew enough to shrug my shoulders and show a slight grin before meandering back into my office.

I just learned another word from the Australian dictionary.

IG inspection coming!
12 Jun 1990 Tuesday

Got some surprising news this morning at the ops meeting. We're getting a visit from the IG (Inspector General) team in late September. The news was about as welcome as a bag of McDonalds French fries at a health food convention.

The DO explained. "You're not gonna like this but the IG is coming. They'll be here in September so I want you all to be ready. That gives us plenty of time. This is a make or break for the commander. If we get a good score; he looks good. If we do poorly, he may lose his job."

Capt Marcus spoke up. He was here for the last inspection and couldn't believe another one was coming up so soon.

"Sir, we just had an IG inspection a short while ago. Don't they normally wait at least 2 years between visits? It's only been a little over a year. Why are they coming back again so soon?"

The DO sensed the frustration in the room, "Listen guys. I know it's a pain in the butt, but the IG's coming. They're going to be at the door in late September so we better be ready. Now, we can look at the short time between inspections as a good thing because we did really well on the last inspection. So our work centers should all be looking pretty good. We should piggyback on the work done at the last inspection and come out of this one looking really good too."

YANKS IN THE OUTBACK

The scuttlebutt about why the IG is so interested in our site - why they're coming back so soon - is because Australia is a sought after destination. They love coming down under. They aren't crazy about coming to Woomera, but they are very excited about stopping off at the exotic locations on the way. Places like Hawaii, Sydney, Fiji, and New Zealand.

So, it looks like Australia – not Woomera - is a sought out destination for the IG folks and the general consensus is that's why they're coming back here so soon.

And, this is not surprising as we've seen similar behavior from other people. They find an excuse to come visit Woomera and then tour around Australia. They come out to the site for an hour long tour and then they're gone; the plane doesn't even have time to shut off the engines and they're back up in the air heading back to Sydney for shopping.

A prime example of this is the weekly MAC flights. Every Wednesday they're scheduled to fly in with supplies from the US. But, it's not unusual for the flight to be cancelled and we have to wait another week or two for the supplies. Cancelling the flight to Woomera is every MAC pilot's mission – they don't like coming here. Their greatest fear is having to overnight in Woomera; worst stop off in Australia. They avoid it at all costs.

I hear the guys in admin joking about how the MAC flights always seem to break down in Richmond - which is just outside of Sydney – but never in Woomera. All it takes for the plane to break down in Sydney is for the pilot to have a runny nose. That means the crew gets an exciting night out and a nice hotel room in one of the premier cities of the world.

But, in Woomera ... it would never happen. The plane could be missing a wing and the pilots would still try to take off and get out of here, "No way were staying in this God forsaken place!"

The admin guys also joke about how the pilots drop off the supplies when they land in Woomera. The pilots keep the engines roaring and when they see that last bit unloaded they close up the doors and fly off.

The MAC crews are so afraid of having to spend any time in Woomera. The admin guys joke about how it's going to get to the point where the plane won't even land; won't even touch the wheels on the tarmac; just push the cargo out the back of the C-5 like a wartime emergency airdrop in a hot landing zone.

And, I live in this place.

But, I disagree with the MAC airlift crews ... I like Woomera. I think it's great and I'm enjoying my time here.

* * *

After the morning meeting I went back to my office and started researching how Sammy did on the last IG inspection. Turns out, he aced it. He received the highest rating of "OUTSTANDING." I figure I'll just leave things as they are; I don't want to fix something that isn't broken; something the last IG team labeled, "outstanding."

GSR: 1st Meeting
13 Jun 1990 Wednesday

We had our first GSR (Ground Station Readiness) meeting today. The commander's conference room was packed with all interested parties - section chiefs, crew commanders, training department, evaluation department, communications department, Aerojet, TRW, Sandia contractors. Everyone seems ready to roll up their sleeves and get to work. The general attitude was one of excitement about getting our second satellite.

The plan is to have at least one meeting a month on the second Wednesday. If we need to schedule more meetings we will. The purpose of the meetings is to see how we're progressing; see if there are any showstoppers; identify any problems; essentially to make sure we're on track to successfully send commands, receive telemetry and perform mission on the new satellite.

The first thing I did was hand out my draft "Action Item" sheet and told everyone to review it and let me know if it makes sense; if it's correct? A few questions came up but for the most part, everyone seemed to be OK with the items and the associated due dates.

I created the action item list by stealing one they used back in Denver for a previous GSR. I got the list from Jack Dubois one of the TRW contractors. He suggested I use it as a starting point.

One of the "big ticket" items on the list is the new spacecraft simulator. Before any commands go to the new spacecraft, they must first be sent to the simulator and pass all the tests. After all, we don't want any "bad" commands going to a live spacecraft.

This action item falls to the software department. Maj Tim Monroe is the Chief of the software department so I asked him, "Do you see any challenges with the new software simulator; getting it up and running and ready for the 'all commands' test?"

"Nah, it won't be a problem," came back his confident and heady reply.

Jack Dubois is a big help to me. He's been in this business since the wheel was invented. He doesn't read the history of the DSP program – he remembers it.

He's been assisting me with putting together the GSR action item list. We started with a list they used in Denver and we just modified it to suit our situation. Some of the items we crossed off straight away because they didn't apply. Others we had to add because they were missing. This is where Jack's memory came in handy as he recalled "bad things" that happened in previous GSRs. We included these "gotchas" to make sure we're ready for the new bird.

Jack is the one who put up the red flag about the software simulator. Apparently, it's a departure from the old simulator in that it's all software based. The old simulator was all hardware; the same hardware as on the spacecraft. So, when you send commands to the old simulator it's exactly the same as sending them to the spacecraft except the simulator is five feet away and the spacecraft is 22 thousand miles away!

We can't use the old simulator with the new spacecraft; they're not compatible. So, we must have the new software simulator up and working prior to receiving the new spacecraft. Jack and TRW have said they will not authorize any commands to the new spacecraft until the "all commands" test has been completed successfully. Therefore, Maj Monroe and his team must have the new simulator ready by the due date.

And, that's why I specifically asked Maj Monroe the question in today's meeting – "Do you see any issues ...?" I want to keep close tabs on the new simulator because it could be a big problem down the road if we can't get it working.

Why the big concern? Again, Jack tipped me off. He told me the new software simulator was giving the guys fits back in Denver. It's not easy to set up and operate. It's a bear. The software guys should be all over it now; asking for docs; going back to Denver to learn how to operate it; rolling up their sleeves and getting their hands dirty trying to figure out how it works.

But, Maj Monroe seems confident. He shrugged off my question about getting the new simulator up and running as if I asked him if he could pour me a cup of hot water. Maybe he knows something I don't know. Maybe it's not as difficult to operate as Jack makes it out to be.

Anyway, I wrote up the meeting minutes and included Maj Monroe's confident reply to document his claim.

I will be tracking the software simulator closely.

Independence Day Parade
4 Jul 1990 Wednesday

Today I lead the US troops for the American Independence Day parade through downtown Woomera.

Last week I got a call from the site commander asking me if I'd like to volunteer for this task. A request from the commander is not really a request; it's more like an order. Of course I accepted and was somewhat glad he thought of me and picked me to do it.

We gathered up in front of the ELDO Hotel and then marched the short distance to Dewrang Ave where we turned right and headed past the reviewing stand.

The reviewing stand was loaded with a bunch of the local high ranking officials and the site commander.

As we passed the stand I called out "eyes right" and then the troops looked right towards the stand and I saluted. The site commander saluted back and then I yelled out "ready front" and the troops snapped their heads to the front and I dropped my salute.

Now, I wasn't looking back to see if the troops were following my commands but from the feedback I received, it all went pretty well. I was relieved when we finally broke ranks and the parade ended. I haven't marched in a long time. Neither have the troops.

GSR: 2nd Meeting
11 Jul 1990 Wednesday

We held our second GSR meeting today. Everyone is still fired up about getting the new spacecraft. We listened to a couple of briefings from the TRW and Sandia contractors about new features and upgrades that are coming.

I addressed each action item asking for status. Are we on-track? Any issues? Any assistance needed to get your action item completed?

Most of the items are fairly straight forward. The work centers are making minor changes/updates to accommodate the new satellite. For instance, the ops guys are making minor changes to their existing procedures. They're main focus is any changes resulting from 2 satellite operations instead of one. And, most of this guidance will come down from the Wing (HQ). They tell me it will only require minor updates to their existing procedures.

I went back to my office and immediately wrote up the meeting minutes. It contains a short summary of what I felt was the most important dialog. And, it includes the action item list with the status given to me at the meeting.

I was pleasantly surprised to hear the positive feedback from the software guys. Maj Monroe says he is having no issues with the new spacecraft simulator. He'll have it up and running and completing the all-commands test will be a breeze. And, I documented his words in the meeting minutes.

When Maj Monroe gave this feedback I glanced over at Jack Dubois (TRW). Jack looked back at me with a shrug of his shoulders. After the meeting I talked to Jack and he told me, "Hey, maybe these software guys are on top of it. I hope they are."

I'm beginning to think Jack is a bit of a worry wart and the new software simulator is not going to be a problem.

Capt Marcus; "The Great Escape"
12 Jul 1990 Thursday

Big buzz after the morning meeting today. Apparently, Capt Marcus is kind of a goat with the other crew commanders because he got away with the equivalent of "murder" in the ops game.

From what I gather, he sent a valid missile launch out via low speed message – a big "no-no." Valid missile launches are supposed to go high speed to give maximum warning time. Low speed messages are essentially left in someone's in-basket and looked at during the next duty day; at least that's my image of what happens!

Also, low speed messages are really only for static stuff like bonfires or other non-moving IR (Infrared) signals. If it's a missile, you're supposed to send it high speed.

Consequently, Headquarters is fuming mad. They're demanding to know why this launch was not sent out high speed and they're calling for Capt Marcus' head on a platter.

But, Capt Marcus is standing on solid ground. For some reason – he felt the launch did not satisfy all the criteria to meet high speed release and therefore he made the decision to send it low speed. And, according to HQ direction, this is always the right call. If you're not sure – send low speed.

Apparently, he had some doubt. It was a borderline call where the crew commander could use best judgment. HQ direction says this judgment call lies squarely with the crew commander. Crew commanders have the discretion to send low speed if they're unsure. HQ even went as far as saying "crew commanders cannot be decertified for sending reports low speed." This gave the crew commanders an out; if in doubt – send low speed. It's the safe thing to do. Headquarters directed that all criteria must be met – no exceptions – so Capt Marcus followed the HQ letter of the law and sent it low speed.

Here's the dilemma for Capt Marcus – if he sends it high speed and he's wrong, he'll be decertified. If he sends it low speed, he can't be decertified. And, decertification for crew commanders is not something you want on your record. So, given these options, which one do you think he's going to pick? It's a no-brainer.

I'm told it was an SRBM (short range ballistic missile) out of Iraq. So, it's a small missile. Our mission here is really to pick up the big ones – ICBMs and SLBM. HQ would be a lot more upset if it was one of these big ones and we sent it out low speed.

The DO wasn't happy with Capt Marcus decision to send this valid launch out low speed. Replay of the tape showed it met all launch criteria but the "motion" wasn't great so Capt Marcus took the safe route by sending low speed. The other crew commanders reviewing the launch on tape were snickering at how Capt Marcus had taken "the safe route" to a new high in lows. They all agreed it should have gone out high speed and cannot see any justification for sending low speed other than to guarantee you don't get decertified.

Even though the DO wasn't happy with Capt Marcus, he still backed him 100%. When HQ called to ask if Capt Marcus had been decertified yet, the DO blasted them.

"On what grounds? He followed your direction to the letter and now you want him decertified? No way. You need to change your ground rules if you want us to send such a launch via high speed, otherwise – when we're less than certain - we'll continue to send low speed. Like you directed, we're only allowed to send high speed if we're 100% sure – you've told us false reports are unacceptable and will not be tolerated. A false report is grounds for decertification.

"But, your direction also says, low speed reports will never result in a decertification; especially for small tactical missiles like the ones out of Iraq and Iran. So, if our crew commanders are not 100% sure, they're going to send low speed. Now if you want us to send all launches like this one high speed – change your rules. My guy knew it was a launch, he wanted to send it high speed but he had second thoughts and didn't want to get it wrong so he took the safe route. He didn't want to get decertified. He knew he could not get decertified by sending low speed, so he did. Now, you're asking me to decertify him – no chance. Like I said, you want us to send high speed – change the rules!"

Apparently, HQ backed down. They agreed, if Capt Marcus followed the HQ directives there's no way he can be decertified.

As far a changing the rules ... HQ backed down on this as well. They are so afraid of the site sending out a false report that they won't go for it; they don't want to take the chance.

A false report is when someone at a site sends a high speed missile warning and then it turns out to be nothing. When this happens, the general who gets woken up in the middle of the night becomes irate. We're told down here at site that when a high speed launch message goes out, we wake up the generals. That's what it's referred to as ... waking up the generals.

HQ is so afraid to wake up the generals for a false report that they want to keep the launch reporting criteria the same even if it means some real launches are missed and sent out via the low speed message traffic.

Crazy!

Common sense says you'd want it the other way around, when it doubt send it high speed, then we'll deal with it from there. But, common sense doesn't seem to be in large quantities when it comes to the military; especially peacetime military operations.

New DO Arrives
23 Jul 1990 Monday

I met the new DO today. He just arrived and is getting a tour of the site. Lt Col French has been gone for a week. They were supposed to have overlap but it didn't happen for some reason. Apparently, the new DO got delayed coming down here and Lt Col French already had orders to go and didn't want to – or couldn't – change them.

The new DO – Maj Reed – just came in from heading up the "trucks" at Holloman AFB in New Mexico. The trucks are a mobile version of what we do here at site. They can be deployed all over the world. I've heard talk about an upcoming deployment to Guam.

Maj Reed seems like a nice guy; very approachable. He's only about five foot nine; balding with a very noticeable scar on his high forehead; relatively slender but doesn't look like someone who works out at the gym.

His background with the Trucks should be a good match for us here; he's familiar with the mission and operations.

IG Inspection – Hide the Books!
27 Jul 1990 Friday

The upcoming IG inspection is causing folks to do some funny stuff. One incident in particular stands out.

Yesterday, I walked into the ops support office and saw SQLDR "Hendo" Henderson standing with a surprised look on his face. He momentarily froze as he saw me come through the door.

It was an awkward scene. Hendo was standing over an open tile in the floor with a stack of notebooks in his hands.

When he realized it was me, he took on a much more relaxed posture.

It's not unusual for me to walk into the ops support office as it's right next door to my office; we're neighbors. My office is more like a hallway, so people pass through it all the time, especially the folks who work in ops support. I return the favor by walking through their office especially if I want to enter the Technical Advisory Group (TAG) area via the back way. So, for me to pop in unexpectedly is really not very unexpected.

He certainly looked guilty standing there with his "you caught me" look and holding a stack of binders with an open floor tile below.

"Oh, Hi Sean," he greeted me with a big exhale letting me know he dodged a bullet. He knows I wouldn't "dob him in", which is Aussie for "snitch on him."

He was more than happy to explain what he was up to.

"Capt Stephens said if the IG sees these documents we're dead; we'll never pass the inspection. So, I offered to help. I told them all we have to do is hide 'em. No worries."

Capt Stephens is the Ops Support Chief.

Hendo continued, "Captain Stephens said, 'We can't do that!' I told him, maybe you can't, but I can! Then I told him and all the other Yanks to leave the office while I take care of the problem."

A big grin formed on my face as the story just kept getting better.

I looked down at the open floor tile and I could feel the strong, cold, air blowing up from the huge floor cavity below.

SQLDR Henderson didn't have to tell me anything more but he did, "I'll put all these folders down here during the inspection. They'll never find 'em. Then when the IG leaves, we'll pull em back up again. Not a problem. The Yanks were all worried about it. As an Aussie I can't get in trouble; I told them to get lost for a while and I'll make the problem go away! "

Then he directed me in a polite yet firm voice, "Now, get out of here!"

I turned and walked back into my office and closed the door behind me. Then I headed for the cafeteria to get a cup of coffee ... laughing out loud the whole way!

PART 3: AUG – OCT 1990

Eclipse Season - No More Mid-Shifts
2 Aug 1990 Thursday

I got some good news today. Maj Reed said there's no need for me to go in every night during the upcoming eclipse season to support the commanding. I was slightly shocked when he told me; in a good way.

He attended the eclipse season briefing I gave to the crews this evening; same briefing I gave last season; same one I used to give back in Denver. The season starts again this month and goes until late October.

He arrived at his decision by asking a few pointed questions, "Sean, you say you're going in every evening to support this commanding. Why?"

"Well sir, Lt Col French said I was his eyes and ears during this critical commanding." I wasn't really confident about my "eyes and ears" role but I assumed Maj Reed would want the same thing.

"So, who does your job while you're off supporting this commanding?"

"I just try to catch up as best I can, when I can." I replied.

"What hands on role do you play in the commanding?"

"None. The GSOs, Aerojet and TRW engineers carry it out"

He had enough information. He made his decision.

"Sean, I want my satellite engineer around when I need him. I want you to stay on days. I don't see any value in having you support this eclipse commanding."

"Yes sir." I replied with a grin reaching from earlobe to earlobe.

Iraq invades Kuwait
3 Aug 1990 Friday

Big news. Iraq invaded Kuwait yesterday. More trouble in the Middle East.

What Team Do You Root For?
7 Aug 1990 Tuesday

I learned another "Aussie" word today. And, I learned it the hard way.

I was hanging out on the ops floor and just happened to enter a conversation about the upcoming college football season. I was telling the guys I'm an Ohio State grad and hope the Buckeyes have a good season.

Then I asked a question that got me in trouble, "What team do you root for?"

As soon as I said that, Australian Squadron Leader (SQDLR) "Hendo" Henderson chimed into the conversation. Prior to my question, he was sitting back deep in his chair with his hands behind his head in a most relaxing position. But, my question brought him out of his restful state.

"Hey mate, I don't know where you come from but here in Australia, we don't root for other people – we do our own rooting."

It seemed like all the guys in the ops area were doubled over laughing before he even finished his sentence – Yanks and Aussies. I knew I had served up a perfect pitch and Hendo had delivered the punch line like a pro but I was lost. I didn't get it.

When the guys finally came to, they filled me in. The word "root" is not used in good company. You never use it when talking about your favorite sports team. You might use it with your mates to describe your attraction to a sexy looking "Shiela" (girl).

To avoid embarrassment in the future I learned how to properly phrase my question to accommodate the Aussie's in the crowd. It involved learning yet another new Aussie word.

Next time I'll ask the question this way, "What team do you barrack for?"

GSR: 3rd Meeting
8 Aug 1990 Wednesday

Had our third GSR meeting today. I opened by giving a short rundown of what we know from headquarters about the launch status. Essentially, everything is on schedule and we should expect no delays in receiving the new satellite.

I especially focused on two critical items. First, the crypto keys. We've got to make sure we've got the correct keys or we're sunk. Apparently, with new satellites in the past, the crypto keys have been a showstopper. I'm told there is a lot of red tape involved and only certain people can authorize their release and only certain people can handle them. If we don't get a jump on it, we'll look pretty silly as a ground station that can't communicate with our new spacecraft. We'll be unable to talk or listen to the new satellite.

Next, the new software simulator. This action item has me a bit stumped. My TRW contractor expert Jack keeps telling me this may become a really big issue. "Sean, they had a hell of a time back in Denver getting this thing to work. The user's manual is bigger than the Bible. It's got lots of capability, but learning how to operate it is not easy. It's going to take a lot of work. I don't see the software guys doing any work on it. They're taking a very easy-going approach and I think they're not going to be able to operate it when we need to run the all-commands test."

Jack followed up with the warning, "TRW will not send any commands to the spacecraft until the all-commands test has been completed successfully."

Actually, TRW doesn't send any commands to the spacecraft; the ground station operators (GSOs) do that. But, all commands are verified by the TRW satellite engineer before transmitting. Therefore, Jack is telling me TRW won't perform their verification function until the all commands test is completed successfully. He wants to test every command on the simulator to verify the new database before sending any of these commands to a live satellite.

To me that sounds fair. We just need to make sure the test is completed prior to our receiving the spacecraft. And, that should be easy.

Why should it be easy?

Because when I asked Maj Monroe at the GSR meeting today for the status of the new spacecraft simulator and the all commands test, he gave me the most positive reply, "No problem."

I pressed him by asking, "You don't see any showstoppers with the new spacecraft simulator and completing the all commands test?"

"None." He stated in an almost deadpan and offhanded way.

I have to admit, I'm a bit concerned about the spacecraft simulator and getting the all commands test completed.

Why?

The Maj seems overconfident to me. He comes across as arrogant.

Jack, from TRW, even spoke up at the meeting saying, "The guys in Denver had a tough time getting the new simulator working. Have you (addressing Maj Monroe) talked to the guys in Denver?"

Maj Monroe's reply was defiant, "We don't need any help from Denver. Our guys at site can handle it. We've got the expertise right here; we don't need any outside help."

The room went quite. We moved onto the next action item.

I made sure to note this dialog in the GSR meeting minutes. I distributed the minutes today with a cover letter. The cover letter lets everyone know they have the opportunity to question what I've written and discuss any changes that need to be made.

I'm wondering if Maj Monroe will contact me to discuss his bold assertions about having the new simulator up and running in time to complete the all commands test. Will he want to challenge what I've written in the minutes; maybe tone down his almost boastful assertions ... maybe come and ask for some help after all?

US Troops Deploying to Saudi Arabia

9 Aug 1990 Thursday

US troops are deploying to Saudi Arabia. It looks like there's going to be a punch up in the Middle East.

IG Inspection: Are You Ready?

13 Aug 1990 Monday

I got called into the Commander's office today. Colonel Benjamin is all worried about the upcoming IG inspection. He wanted to know what I'm doing to get ready for it.

I told him the truth, "Nothing."

He wasn't thrilled with my answer.

"All the other sections are working 14 hours days and you're doing nothing - how come? He asked with a lot of displeasure in his voice.

"Well, sir, we just had an IG inspection only a short time ago and my predecessor Capt Jenks got an Outstanding; can't get any higher than that. Why would I go and change anything? I figure if the setup was 'Outstanding' last time why wouldn't it be this time?"

The Commander seemed to accept my logic. He couldn't find any fault with it but he had to get in the last words, "Well, you better be right. I'm expecting an 'Outstanding' again this time."

I feel the whole IG inspection is a waste of time. Even if Capt Jenks had gotten only a 'Satisfactory' last time, I still wouldn't do anything different.

I look at the IG inspection the same way I used to look at dormitory room inspections – my room is ready all the time for inspection.

You can pop in anytime and inspect. The room's ready. I don't just clean it when you tell me you're coming; it's clean all the time.

Well, I look at my work center the same way. This is how I run it, it's working, if you want to inspect me, come on and do it. If you see something or some process that can be improved, I'm willing to listen and consider doing it that way. If I'm doing something dumb – let me know and I'll start doing it the smart way.

But, let's face it; the IG inspection team is a first class joke! It's not that the guys aren't smart or that they aren't good troops, it's much more simple and basic than that. The whole process is fundamentally stupid; a first class waste of taxpayer money; a colossal boondoggle!

How can I make these claims with such authority?

Easy, I've been through many IG inspections before – I've seen it first-hand. Let's look at some basics here.

How is the IG team supposed to inspect me when they don't even know what I do or how I do it? They don't know my job. Yes, they have a description of what I do but that's it; they don't know how to do it.

Having the IG team inspect my work center is as ridiculous as having me inspect an air-conditioning installation work center. I don't know the first thing about installing air conditioners! I would get laughed out of the work center. They would physically kick me off the premises.

Too bad we can't do that with the IG team, although I have recommended it in private to several of my fellow officers. Let's greet them at the gate with a howitzer in full blaze! They thought I was joking.

To me the IG team is another government/military jobs program. Get more and more people in the service doing more and more non-value adding activities. Keep stacking the red tape - red tape on top of red tape. Just keep stacking it until the whole system collapses.

Brother's Wedding
14 Aug 1990 Tuesday

Not sure how I did it but the boss is letting me go back to the States for a little over a week to attend my twin brother Sam's wedding. I wasn't planning on going. I figured I'd never get the time off. So, I didn't even bother asking. But, my Mom called and convinced me to at least ask. So, I did. Boss said ok. I'm leaving this weekend, back on the 28th.

Back from US
28 Aug 1990 Wednesday

Left my diary in Woomera so haven't written anything since my trip to the States for my brother's wedding. I suppose that's OK since I'm keeping this journal for the purpose of documenting my experience here in Australia – a "Yank in the Outback" so to speak.

Dave Ives

IG Inspection: Misplaced Priorities
4 Sep 1990 Tuesday

The upcoming IG inspection is causing some people to have misplaced priorities. I observed this first hand at the morning meeting today.

The Aerojet contractor asked for some offline tape time to fine tune our ground processing computers for detecting the SCUD missiles coming out of Iraq. The idea is to be ready if/when Iraq starts firing their SCUDs in anger. The tension is building up for a fight to "free" the Kuwaitis. Every day it looks more and more likely that the US is planning to go ahead with an attack. Saddam is not backing down.

The request for tape time met with extreme resistance by Capt Marcus from the training department.

"There's no way I'm giving up any offline tape time. I need every bit of this time to get in extra training so we can get an outstanding grade for the upcoming IG inspection," he stated in an "I ain't backing down" tone of voice. He was dead serious, essentially telling everyone that his grade in the upcoming IG inspection was the highest priority – even higher than getting ready for any possible upcoming military conflict.

He sounded very silly, defending his training time; bureaucracy at its best. It's all about my career – forget the guys on the ground in Iraq or Kuwait who may be relying on our systems. Forget about doing everything we can to get ready for real life warfighting capability. Instead, let's focus on our careers; our checklists. Let's focus on making the IG team happy. Let's get the IG team to like us; give us a good grade; even though they have no idea what we do or how we do it. Even though the IG is totally focused on red tape and timewasting peacetime protocol all of which are virtually useless at an operational site and especially during a time of war.

I'm extrapolating here about war because I've never been in a war ... but there are plenty of historical lessons showing the military must make the switch from peacetime ops to wartime ops; the sooner the switch the better. The longer the switch takes the higher the risk of losing lots of soldiers and maybe even the war.

Battleship Washington Story

A great example of this is found in the book, "Battleship at War; the Epic Story of the USS Washington" by Ivan Musicant. The sailors go from peacetime operations to a wartime footing almost instantly.

The way it happens is magic.

The ship is underway in the Atlantic and the captain wants to test his crew. He sends out the command for "battle stations" but doesn't tell the crew it's only a drill.

All battle stations report back ready in record time. The previous fastest time is eight minutes; the crew did it this time in four and half minutes.

The Captain is pleased but also amazed. How could the crew beat the previous record by three and half minutes? Impossible.

Normally a crew member must run to the bridge to get the key to unlock the ammo store. This time, not one crew member came up to get a key.

The Captain inspected the battle stations and found the same infraction at each one – the locked ammo doors had been pried open with a crow bar! The crews made a wartime decision – forget the key; break the lock, open the door and get the ammo – NOW!

The Captain approved this crew initiated change in procedure and immediately adopted it. No more locks on the ammo room doors! No more sending a runner to the bridge to sign for the key! No more useless peacetime military bureaucratic BS!

No more peace time nonsense rules and regulations. Time to play for keeps!

The ship had converted to a war time footing.

*** * * ***

And, I can see we are experiencing a similar peacetime dilemma. We have folks who place their career path on a higher footing than getting ready to support troops in the battle zone.

At the meeting this morning, I was glad to see Capt Marcus' get challenged by Lt Ethan Kelly (Australian Navy).

"I'm sorry but I don't understand. Somebody's asking for tape time to figure out how we can optimize our detection capabilities for SCUD launches out of Iraq, but you don't want to give up any of your training time because it impacts on your getting a good grade for the upcoming IG inspection? Are you serious?"

I was surprised by Capt Marcus when he responded, "Do you want me to fail the IG inspection? I've got to have that tape time to get an outstanding grade."

It was as if he didn't even listen to Lt Kelly. Capt Marcus seems totally focused on his career.

Maj Reed stepped into the fray, "Are you telling me we have guys on the floor who are not qualified or guys who have not been certified; guys who shouldn't be on the ops floor?"

"No sir. Every person on crew is certified. We always keep up with certification. But, in order to get an outstanding on the upcoming IG we need to show a higher than minimum standard. To get an outstanding we need every bit of this tape time to show our crews get additional training above and beyond the standard," Capt Marcus defended his position.

"In other words, you don't really need this tape time; it's for extra training only?"

"Sir, I looked at the results of the previous IG inspection and the reason we didn't get an outstanding is because we didn't do extra training. I've got to do this extra training if we want to get an outstanding from the IG."

Maj Reed made his ruling, "Capt Marcus, I want you to give the Aerojet guys the tape time they need. Then you do your additional training with what's left. You let me worry about the IG if they give you any grief for not meeting some additional standard of excellence."

Common sense won out. I have a lot of respect for Maj Reed; but my respect just went up another notch.

Optimize Ground Station for SCUD
8 Sep 1990 Saturday

Karl Henry the lead Aeroject contractor engineer came in this morning to perform some offline analysis. This is the tape time slot he got from Capt Marcus. Capt Marcus wouldn't budge on giving up any tape time during the week but instead gave up a two hour Saturday morning slot. Karl grabbed it.

I find it rather strange that Capt Marcus would put up a fight for Saturday morning tape time; I don't think they ever use their weekend slots. Why he put up such a stink about giving up tape time I'll never understand; especially when this tape time is in support of the military build-up – and possible war - in the Middle East.

Anyway, Karl used this precious tape time to optimize our ground station processing for detecting the Iraqi SCUD missiles.

We've already got a lot of experience with the SRBMs – short range ballistic missiles - from Iran/Iraq War. We've got virtually all of these launches saved in our tape library. Karl will use these old tapes to determine the best way to optimize our ground station for detecting these types of launches.

GSR: 4th Meeting
12 Sep 1990 Wednesday

GSR has become a bit ho-hum as we're confident we are ready. Almost all action items have been completed. The only big ticket item still outstanding is the "all commands" test. But, my software department "experts" tell me it's all under control.

Pointer Program
13 Sep 1990 Thursday

I've been working on a computer program for the last week or so to predict when our ground station antennas will be able to "see" the new satellite. I wrote it in BASIC.

The program computes the ground antenna pointing angles for a given geosynchronous satellite sub-point location. So, if you give me the sub-point for a geo-sync satellite, I can compute where the ground antenna should point to see it – azimuth and elevation angles.

This program came about as a result of embarrassment. You see, back in Denver, my boss asked us engineers to figure out how far we could move a satellite west before our ground antennas couldn't see it anymore. None of us could do it.

So, from that embarrassing situation, I decided to study this problem and then come up with a program to calculate the answer. I was determined to create such a program. That way, if ever asked again, I wanted to be able to answer, "No problem Sir. Let me bring up my program. Ok, here it is ... we'll lose the bird at 'so-and-so' degrees longitude."

Well, I'm using the program now to chunk out the elevation angles for our ground station antennas against varying sub-point locations. Then I plotted these numbers. The result gives me an easy to read reference for sub-point vs elevation angle. I can look at the plot and see the sub-point where our ground antennas should pick up the new satellite.

I've posted this sub-point vs elevation angle plot prominently on my bulletin board above my desk for easy reference.

The final step is to read the "mass predicts" which is a huge binder of tables showing the location of the satellite at any given time. It's generated in Sunnyvale and shipped out to us via the mail.

We won't receive the mass predicts until after the satellite is launched and it's in geosync orbit.

The launch is scheduled for late Oct but they're experiencing some issues so we're expecting the launch date to slip.

IG Inspection: "We're here to help"
19 Sep 1990 Wednesday

The IG team arrived on Monday. I got inspected yesterday. A Captain "So and So" (can't remember his name) looked at my books. He greeted me in a most friendly manner. He's a red headed guy a little older looking than me, in great shape and immaculate uniform presentation and grooming - a classic IG inspector.

I thought, "This is going to be great. He'll see the same stuff from the last IG inspection and give me an outstanding grade just like Sammy got. We're going to get along just fine and this is going to go very smoothly. No problem."

I was wrong.

I was surprised as he challenged me about my checklist items, "Why have you written it this way? It's in passive voice. It tells you right here in regulation – blah, blah; Volume blah, blah - your checklists should be in active voice."

I couldn't believe what I was hearing. How do I answer? Do I answer truthfully or do I play the game and humor him. Do I say what's really on my mind or do I conger up some Air Force correct jargon to make this guy happy and more importantly, to make him go away?

What did I want to say? What was I really thinking? Well, here are a few ideas that went through my mind ...

"You came all the way from the US to tell me that?"

"Haven't you got something better to do?"

"Are you that bored?"

"Are you for real?"

"Why are you here?

But, that's not what I said. Instead I opted for the more civilized approach, the approach that would hopefully lead to a happy – for me – ending.

"Well, you see sir, that's the way my predecessor had it written up and he got an 'outstanding' grade during the last recent IG inspection. I figured it must be right otherwise he wouldn't have gotten such a high grade. I also figured it would not be wise to change something that worked really well for the last IG inspection."

My attempt to get the inspector to change his mind didn't work. He wasn't interested in previous IG inspections or what my predecessor did. He was interested in the here and now.

"The regulation clearly states the checklists must be in active voice. So, it looks like the last IG inspector didn't catch it. As it sits right now, I have no choice but to give you a failing mark."

I struggled with his logic. This guy is going to fail me because some stupid checklist – a checklist I never use; no one uses – is written in passive voice?

This checklist only exists in case the IG comes to town. That's it. I never use it. I've never seen anyone use it or ask for it except the IG.

What is this "all so important" checklist?

It's what's called a "Self-Inspection" checklist. And it's full of questions that go something like this ...

> *"Have you checked and secured the office safe before going home for the day?"*

> *"Have you checked off all your self-inspection items for the day?"*

And, on and on it goes with more and more embarrassingly stupid and idiotic questions.

Now, I'm getting penalized for the way my checklist is written. The items are all there but he doesn't like the way they are phrased.

He gave me an offer I couldn't refuse, "If you rewrite all your checklists tonight, I can give you a Satisfactory, otherwise I have to fail you. Are you willing to re-write all your checklists tonight in active voice and have it ready for tomorrow?"

"Yes, sir!" I shot back.

"Ok, I'll see you tomorrow morning first thing. If you have all these checklists corrected, I'll give you a SAT; that's the highest grade I can give you since your checklists need to be corrected. If the checklists were in active voice I could give you an 'outstanding' based on all the other aspects of your shop."

So, last night I took home a pile of checklists and got out a red pen and started the exciting process of re-writing the checklists to active voice. The IG inspector said it was OK to use a red pen and cross out the old checklist item and underneath it write the new one.

I sat at my round dining room table until midnight re-writing the checklists. I would take my red pen and cross out the old checklist item – for example –

> ~~Have you checked and secured the office safe before going home for the day?~~

And, then write below it in red ink …

> *At the end of the duty day, check to make sure the safe is securely locked.*

I did this for about 100 checklist items … all equally useless and virtually meaningless; all just to satisfy another IG inspector who has no business inspecting my work center.

Now all these checklist items will sit inside their binders never seeing the light of day until the next IG inspection comes along.

This morning I met with my friendly IG inspector Captain and he reviewed my rewritten checklists and then gave me his verdict, "If these checklists looked like this when I arrived, I would have given you an outstanding. The regulation clearly states your checklists must be in active voice, so you should have read the reg and then phrased your checklist items in active voice. Now, I could have failed you but instead I'll give you a SAT but that's the highest mark I can give since I had to ask you to redo your checklists. Ok?"

I stared at him with a dazed look. I couldn't believe he was serious. All I could think of was, "You came all the way down here to the outback of Australia just to scold me for not having my checklists in active voice? The United States government must have way too much money if they can spend it on useless activities like this!"

But, my response was more measured; I simply refocused my eyes from a dazed look to an "I'm back" look and quietly said, "Ok."

I just wanted my red-headed friend to leave. Go away. Go back to wherever you came from and take your silly IG mentality with you.

* * *

The whole situation is so ridiculous it's difficult for me to talk about it without feeling foolish. When I talk about the IG inspection, I feel like someone talking about a topic that's completely useless.

For instance, how would you feel about talking to someone about the color of dust? How exciting would that be? And, how would you like to talk about it for hours and hours? And, write a report on it? And, give a briefing on it? And, make someone redo their checklists because the dust color observing criteria is not written in active voice?

Insanity!

Yet, that's what the IG inspection feels like to me. Everyone is so serious about an activity that so useless; so manpower draining; so non-value adding; so STUPID!

Now, could the IG inspection be of value?

I suppose. But, that's not how it's done. It's just a jobs program where people go through the motions of making themselves look important and adding no real value. Instead they do the opposite, they drain value; they make things worse; they disrupt operations; they demoralize; they cause people to tell lies – lot of lies; just to get the good grade. Just so everyone thinks everything is OK ... when really it's not.

The standard IG joke goes like this ...

The two biggest lies in the Air Force happen when the IG inspector meets the local commander and they make this exchange.

<u>Biggest lie number 1:</u>
IG Inspector: "Hello, we're here to help!"

<u>Biggest Lie number 2:</u>
Local Commander: "Boy, are we glad to see you!"

And, the lies just continue on from there ...

* * *

I think a better question for the IG to ask me would go something like this ...

"Is your position adding any value to the operation?"

I would have a hard time justifying my role here at site. And, that would be the case for a lot of the military guys here. It seems to me the military overstaffs everything; except for areas where critical staff is needed – like warfighters.

The IG inspection has cemented my feelings that my position here at site is not needed. After all, the IG simply inspected my checklists and binders to see if they're in compliance with regulations. The IG made no inspection of what I actually do; what work I do day in and day out. They made no attempt to ask other work centers about how my work affects and/or supports their work center. The IG inspectors never asked me what I do to support operations. They couldn't care less. They're not interested. They are simply paper-pushers. They are the "red ink" brigade; going around to different sites goofing off and having a good time while away from their home base on fat TDY pay.

Can you tell I'm not a fan of the IG?

Ultralight Crash

22 Sep 1990 Saturday

Just got back from a BBQ at one of the Aerojet contractor's house. Ben was having a few people by and so he invited me. I got to meet his wife Rita and all the kids.

Ben must really be in love. Rita and her 5 children came as a package deal when Ben signed on to become the new husband. He seems very happy about the whole situation.

Ben is a shift worker for Aerojet. I normally don't get invited to contractor gatherings, so I feel a bit honored to get an invite. Ben and I get along pretty well and I think he invited me because it's the neighborly thing to do.

Here in Woomera things are pretty casual. People seem less guarded; more friendly. They take on a more laid back approach to life. I like it.

But, during the BBQ some very sad news started circulating. That's another thing about Woomera, news travels fast. We heard that one of our troops crashed in an ultralight accident and died. It's Sgt Jones. He works in the PowerStation. I've seen him around the site but I don't know him. He's a small blonde haired guy in his late twenties or so I'd guess.

I know his wife better. They just recently got married. She's Fiona the cleaning lady. The same gal who got upset because I tracked mud all over here freshly mopped floor. The one who complained to Lt Col French and then I apologized to avert an international incident.

IG Grade: Commander Scolds Me
24 Sep 1990 Monday

I got called into the commander's office to explain my poor grade from the IG inspection.

He wasn't pleased, "How come you only got a SAT? I thought you assured me you had everything under control and you were ready. A SAT is just one step above flunking."

I took a deep breath and then answered, "Captain Jenks got an outstanding during the last IG inspection only a little over a year ago. I decided the best approach was to leave everything alone and go with a winning formula. Well, it turns out an outstanding last time is only a satisfactory this time. The inspector didn't like my self-inspection checklists – the same checklists that got Sammy an outstanding during the last IG inspection. My checklists are written in passive voice and the regs say they're supposed to be in active voice. The IG inspector said he could flunk me but gave me an out. He said if I redo all the checklists in active voice he'd pass me with a minimum SAT grade. I took him up on the offer."

The commander rolled his eyes and paused as he tried to think of something to say in response. He then seemed to give up before finally muttering, "Oh all right. But, I was counting on you to get an outstanding and then when I saw the final report showing only a SAT, I was shocked. I wasn't worried about your work center but I guess I should have been. The work centers I worried about came back with outstanding grades. They worked 14 hours days and it paid off. Whereas you seemed to be unconcerned about the IG and now your grade reflects the effort you put in."

He tried to make me feel bad and it worked for a moment until I came to my senses and realized he's just playing the game too. The commander wants a good IG score to boost his career. Who cares if the whole exercise is a waste of time; waste of taxpayer money; waste of resources? Let's all just play the game.

I felt very good about my IG score. I felt it represented maximum efficiency. Let them come into town and tell me what it is they want; then I do it and get out with a passing score.

What if I had worked hours and hours trying to get everything just right only to have my red-headed IG friend tell me the same thing, "Your checklists are wrong!"

Forget it. I liked the way I did it. Here's all my useless checklists and binders, let me know if there's anything wrong.

The commander looked at me like I ruined his career.

Summary Courts Officer: Assigned
25 Sep 1990 Tuesday

Sarah, the commander's secretary, rang me this morning and said, "Sean, the commander wants to see you right now."

"Really, I just saw him yesterday, what's this about?" I asked in a surprised voice.

"Not sure, but he wants to see you now. Get down here," she stopped the conversation and left me hanging.

I got up from my desk and started walking to the commander's office.

I started thinking, "I never get called to see the commander. Now, this will be two days in a row. I wonder if he wants to chew me out some more about the IG inspection."

Colonel Benjamin is a pretty nice guy; almost too nice. He's very soft spoken and never seems to get outwardly upset. He's as skinny as a starving POW. He's got blond hair combed over to the side in an untidy fashion. He seems to carry this constant worried look. Even when he smiles it looks like he's not sure if he should.

Sarah, his Australian secretary, has confided in me from time to time. Once while chatting with her she confessed a pet peeve she has with the commander which gives some insight into his personality.

"He tries so hard to fit in. Sometimes it's too embarrassing. Like when he tries to speak Australian. You know how we say "barbie" for BBQ and "breakie" for breakfast? Well, he comes up with his own. For instance, we have the "Hail and Farewell" parties to greet all the new people and send off the old. Well you know what he calls them?

"Hailies and Farewellies!"

I don't know how to get him to stop doing that. It sounds ridiculous. I can't stand it. If he says it again, I'm gonna tell him. I'll tell him nicely but I'm going to let him know just how stupid that sounds to Australians. And I'll bet the Americans think it's silly as well!"

I walked into the Commander's office and he told me to take a seat. Then he gave me the low-down, "Lt Mitchell ...

I knew it wasn't something good when he started by calling me Lt Mitchell and not my first name.

"Lt Mitchell, I've selected you to be my Summary Courts Officer."

My first thoughts ... "What's that?"

He continued, "You are the United States Air Force representative to the family of Sgt Jones who became deceased in the ultralight accident last Saturday afternoon."

As I looked closer at him, it appeared he was reading something hidden in his hands below the back of the desk. I felt like I was at the police station and the cops were reading me my rights. All seemed very legal.

The Commander had more to say, "I want you to devote all your time to this task. I've spoken with Maj Reed and he knows you've been assigned as my Summary Courts Officer. He knows you'll be working for me until this whole thing is wrapped up. The best thing you can do is to keep a detailed diary of everything. That way you can defend yourself if the family decides to take any legal action against the Air Force."

He gave me the phone number of some guy at Clark Air Base in the Philippines. This guy will be my point of contact. I'm supposed to listen to him and do what he says. If I do, then I should be alright.

He finished up by saying, "This is a very important job. Your top priority – your only priority – is your Summary Courts Officer duties. I don't want to see you in this building until this is over. I don't know how long it will take; it doesn't matter. Do you understand?"

I sat there stunned for a moment. Then I let out a big gulping sound followed by an unconvincing, "Yes sir."

Summary Courts Officer: Done and Dusted

30 Sep 1990 Sunday

It appears that my Summary Courts Officer days are numbered. What I mean is it looks like it's all done and dusted. It's all been moving quite fast.

The Air Force appears to be pretty good at this thing; they've got the procedures in place which makes the process fairly straight forward.

First thing I did last Tuesday when I got assigned this task is call my contact at Clark Air Base. He was a big help. He gave me a list of things to do and he also gave me the warning, "You don't want to screw this up. It's one of the few opportunities in your Air Force career where – if you screw up – you could end up in Leavenworth." He also told me to keep a written diary and document, document, document. "Oh boy," I thought to myself, "This is nuts."

Anyway, I got a small black book and it became my Summary Courts Officer diary. I'm writing down everything. As of today, it's probably got 50 pages of writing. I write down who I talk to, what we talk about, where we talk, the time we talk, what we had to drink. I write it all down.

Per my Clark Air Base friend's advice and checklist I carried out the following:

1. Collected and accounted for Sgt Jone's personal effects from his work center – the powerhouse.
2. Visited Sgt Jone's wife Fiona – the very same lady I apologized to a while back when I stomped my muddy boots all over her newly mopped floor. I went to her house and we sat at the kitchen table. TSgt Winters from the Satellite Readout Station (SRS) was there. I guess he was supporting her during her time of grief. It didn't appear to me that Fiona was too upset about the whole situation. But, I'm not sure how someone is supposed to act after such a devastating event. Maybe it was just her defense mechanism to act casual about it. I asked her the questions I got from my contact in the Philippines. Essentially, finding out her wishes and explaining what Air Force burial benefits are available.
3. I then called the Philippines and relayed the information. He took it from there.
4. Next thing you know, last Friday, we received an official message (I didn't see it) explaining everything. Col Benjamin briefed me. The body will be flown out to the USA for burial in his hometown. Fiona will be flying out to attend the funeral in the USA. TSgt Winters will be going along with Fiona as a chaperone.

When I got off the phone with my Clark Air Base contact last Friday afternoon, he told me my official duties as Summary Courts Officer are essentially over. There may be a few mopping up duties to perform but for the most part I'm "out of the woods" (his words.) I guess that means my Air Force career is still intact.

GSR: 5th Meeting
10 Oct 1990 Wednesday

Monthly GSR meeting this morning went well. There's a bit more excitement in the air because the new satellite is scheduled for launch early next month.

I'm ticking off completed action items like crazy. There's a sense of confidence that it's all going to come off without a hitch.

I'm still concerned about the 'all commands test.' I'll be relieved when that action item is completed. Maj Monroe was his usual confident self, "Lt Mitchell, we've got it under control. We'll have it done in time for your new satellite. Don't worry."

I don't understand why he doesn't just do it. Why wait? His main excuse is it's not a priority for him; his guys have more important things to do than work on a new satellite. They're busy enough with the old satellite. And, besides, it's an easy action item and it won't take long to complete and therefore what's the rush.

Again, I noted all this in the meeting minutes I distributed to all the work centers today.

PART 4: NOV 1990 – JAN 1991

Flight 15 Launch
13 Nov 1990 Tuesday

Flight 15 launched successfully from Florida this morning at about 10:00 local time. We've been talking about it and preparing for months but now the baby is born; it's coming our way.

We received an incoming message telling us its current location and its drift rate – three degrees per day westward. It'll be coming to us via the Pacific Ocean.

Based on this info we should be able to see it from our ground station in late December. This is when the satellite sub-point reaches our ground antenna eastern limit of around 216 degrees East Longitude (~144 West longitude). So, we should be able to track it just before it reaches Hawaii.

I'm guessing we won't pick up the satellite until our ground antenna elevation angle is above three degrees or so. This happens a few days after the satellite passes our eastern limit. So I figure we should pick up the bird just after Christmas, say 28 or 29 Dec.

I passed this on to the SRS guys. These are the guys who operate our ground antennas. They plan to be looking for the bird four or five days earlier just to be on the safe side. Who knows; maybe we can pick up the bird at very low elevation angles – less than three degrees?

We need to have our ground station readiness (GSR) action items completed well before the satellite reaches our eastern viewing limit. So far, we're on-track except for the "all commands test." But, the software guys keep assuring me it's in the bag; nothing to worry about. I'm looking forward to the time when I can look back at this and laugh "... it all came together brilliantly, what was I so worried about?"

GSR Meeting: Are we ready?

14 Nov 1990 Wednesday

The GSR meeting today took on a new energy. Now that Flight 15 is successfully launched and in orbit, we realize it really happening; it's really coming; we're really getting a brand new satellite. And, we better be ready or we're going to look awfully foolish; we'll have a lot of egg on our face.

And, I – as the GSR coordinator – will take most of the blame if it doesn't come together.

That's ok. I've been in situations like this before; situations where I have all the responsibility but hardly any authority; situations where if it all goes bad – I get hammered. But, on the other hand – if it all goes well – I'm just doing my job.

I approach my role as the GSR coordinator this way ... I'll do my best. If my best isn't good enough, then so be it. If my strategy; my approach; my method isn't up to scratch, then I'll accept the consequences; I'll accept the blame.

I believe in people. If I can just get everyone to take on a good teamwork attitude, I feel everything will work out; everything will come together.

After all, there's no way I can perform all the tasks that need to be done. I don't have the time, or the energy, or the expertise. For me to go around trying to do everyone's job would be disastrous. Yet, I've seen people try to do this. It never works. So, my approach is to encourage, "You can do it. Good job. Have we forgotten anything? Do you need assistance with that task? What can I do to remove any roadblocks?"

The strategy/approach has worked well for me in the past. I trust it. I'll go with it.

One such occasion comes to mind.

Combined Federal Campaign (CFC) at Buckley

I got the call one day; the dreaded call. The call no junior officer wants to get.

I sat in front of the commander's desk and he said, "You're going to be my CFC officer this year."

My heart stopped.

CFC stands for Combined Federal Campaign. It's the special duty nobody wants. It usually goes to some lowly unsuspecting lieutenant. I fit that description; I got the job.

The year before, my officemate – another lieutenant - got the assignment. I saw what happened to him. After his experience, all the junior officers were deathly afraid to get stuck with the CFC.

His transgression was unforgivable. At least that's how the commander felt.

What did he do wrong?

He didn't reach the financial goal set by the base commander – a general – at Lowry AFB. So, the general called our commander at Buckley ANGB and chewed him out. Our commander then called my office mate and chewed him out.

The CFC had officially ended but my officemate was ordered to go around to every work center – again – and ask for more money. And, he was told to keep doing it until the CFC financial goal – set by the general at Lowry – was met.

It was a disaster. I felt so bad for my officemate. I was so glad it wasn't me.

The next year, I got my turn in the hot seat. The commander gave me very simple instructions, "I don't care what you do, but I better not get a phone call from the general at Lowry!"

Those were my marching orders.

The first thing I found out was I had the biggest group. How big?

Well, I attended the kick-off CFC meeting in downtown Denver and the friendly lady facilitator asked everyone in the room to say their name and how many in their group. So, I sat at the table dumbfounded as I listened to numbers ...

Beth Jones, Training, 10 people.

Brad Burns, Production Centre, 8 people.

Bill Schwartz, Lowry HQ Admin, 28 people (He got a gasp and a clap because he had so many people in his group.)

Blah, blah, blah ... then it was my turn.

Lt Mitchell, Buckley Group, 750 people!

When the meeting ended I left with a bit of a chip on my shoulder ... how come the lowly lieutenant gets 750 people?

I called a kick-off meeting with all the Buckley work center representatives. The conference room was packed as I explained my approach. I had a very simple goal; one that everyone in the room could achieve. It had nothing to do with the general at Lowry's goal; it was my goal.

I told all the work center representatives that if they achieved this goal they had nothing to worry about, I'll take the heat if the general gets upset. Also, I told them there will be no going around to the work centers a second time like last year; that won't happen. I won't do it and I won't ask them to do it.

Then I hit them with the goal, "I want you to personally present the CFC paperwork to each person in your work center and then ask them if they'd like to contribute."

I continued, "There is no minimum amount they need to contribute. There's no amount they have to contribute based on their rank. They don't have to give a dime if they don't want to. All I'm asking you to do is contact them – and ask them – personally. That's it.

"If you contact each and every person in your work center personally about the CFC, you've hit your goal. Can you all do that? Can you personally talk to each person in your work center? Is there anything stopping you from doing that?"

I looked around the conference room at all the relieved faces. Course they could do that. They seemed happy at not having to reach some goofy – pressure cooker - dollar amount goal.

My plan was to offer each person a chance to donate – voluntarily – to the CFC. If we didn't raise enough money for the general at Lowry – tough! I didn't care. I wasn't going to be part of forcing people to donate.

I held a progress meeting a week later and just about every work center rep had completed the goal – they presented and talked to everyone in their work center – personally – about the CFC.

And, much to my surprise, the dollars were flowing. This was a very accidental side benefit to my approach. I thought folks would be so upset about last year they wouldn't give anything this year. But, according to the feedback from the work center representatives, people were giving more this year because no one was forcing them to give. And, they were giving more because someone took the time to come up and talk to them personally about giving.

I was shocked to see the big CFC money thermometer each morning showing more and more money. I have no idea who updated the thermometer every day but it was pretty exciting seeing more and more red paint get splatted on to show the new level.

Finally, I drove in one morning and the thermometer was completely red – we hit the financial goal. Not my goal – the one set by the general at Lowry.

The final tally came out to a crazy number – we blew away the goal by a mile. I got congratulated by our commander, "Great job Mitch, I never got a call from the general – except to congratulate me on reaching our CFC Buckley Group goal."

I learned a big lesson from this experience. Treat people well and they respond well. We treated our Buckley Group folks with respect, "Please consider donating to the CFC; whatever amount feels comfortable for you." And, they responded in kind; they were generous beyond all expectations.

And - tying this back to the GSR effort - I'm treating the GSR team the same way; I'm treating them with respect. And, I'm looking for a similar result; they'll deliver in a big way.

We'll see if my approach works.

Flight 15 - When can we see it?
21 Nov 1990 Wednesday

The folks at Sunnyvale sent us our first set of "mass predicts" for the new satellite - Flight 15. The mass predicts give us a time vs location for the satellite.

My pointer program tells me our ground antennas should see the new bird when it crosses 216 East longitude (144 West). Reading the mass predicts, this happens late Christmas Day.

But, when the satellite crosses 216 degrees longitude our ground antennas will be at zero degrees elevation so I predict we won't see the new satellite until a few days later, say 28 Dec. That's when our ground antenna elevation angles are higher - about three degrees - which sounds more reasonable.

SCUD Launch; Iraqi Test
3 Dec 1990 Monday

Saddam launched a few SCUD missiles yesterday. It was early morning Baghdad time; about 10 am local. Our crews detected them. Looks like he's performing a few tests as the missiles stayed within Iraqi boundaries. This will give us more data so we can tweak our systems to better detect SCUDs if and when he decides to use them in anger.

The Aerojet guys are already jumping on it. They'll work closely with the ops crews to make sure we optimize our setup to detect SCUD launches.

Our primary mission is to detect big ICBM launches, not these small SCUD missiles. But, with things heating up in the Middle East, it looks like these small missiles may start taking on a much higher priority.

GSR Meeting: Software Puts Best Guy on Job

5 Dec 1990 Wednesday

GSR meeting today was a bit tense. We moved it up one week. Normally, it's the second Wednesday of the month. I felt we needed to get together sooner as time is getting short and I want to avoid any last minute "gotchas."

The satellite is in orbit. It's drifting our way. It'll be within view of our ground station in a little over three weeks (if my calculations are correct).

And yet, there's still one big outstanding task on our action item list. It's that nagging "all commands test."

Maj Monroe was full of assurances as usual. "Don't worry. We'll get the new simulator running and we'll complete the test. It's not going to be a problem. I'm putting my best guy on the task next week. He'll be dedicated to getting the simulator up and running. He's got no other duties; he'll be focused on that one task alone. So, it's as good as done."

I wasn't convinced. "You've been telling me for the last several months that you are on top of this action item, now you're telling me you still need to figure it out? What if your best guy can't get it done next week? What's the backup plan?"

He hit me with another one of his condescending speeches, "We have other work to do besides your GSR action items. We don't just drop all our other tasks to work on your stuff. Our time and manpower is limited. We work tasks based on priority – your GSR stuff has not been a priority. I told you I'm putting my best guy on the task next week. It's going to be his sole assignment; he won't have any other tasks to distract him. We'll have it done. So relax."

I'd heard it before; just another excuse. I tried to insert myself into the process by offering some assistance, "Well, is there anything we can do to assist you guys? Do you want me to get in touch with the Denver guys to see if they can help?"

Maj Monroe started getting testy. "We've got it. The guys in Denver can't help us. We can handle it. We don't need any help."

I hope he's right and I'm just getting worried for nothing. But, based on his past assurances, I'm beginning to lose faith in this guy.

Software: "We can't do it"
17 Dec 1990 Monday

I got cornered in my office today. It was a surprise visit from Maj Monroe and his "best guy" Capt Stan Kendall. They came to tell me the bad news, "We can't get the new simulator running."

I was shocked but I shouldn't have been. I somehow knew this day was coming; the day of reckoning; the day of truth.

These two guys surrounded and stood over me as they formed an excuse making tag-team.

Maj Monroe started, "I had Stan on this task for the last week. He spent over 60 hours working it and couldn't get it done. If my best guy can't do it – then it can't be done."

Then the "best guy" chimed in, "Sean, it's too convoluted. It's not worth doing. The new simulator is a piece of junk. The Air Force should get our money back. It's a useless piece of software. It's so antiquated and has code that no one uses; they don't even support it anymore."

I thought he was going to go on forever with his excuse list.

I think it's appropriate at this juncture to give a brief description of these two characters.

Maj Monroe is on the heavy set side, has a roundish face and a commanding, confident presence. But, when he speaks he sends out a conflicting message; his speech doesn't match his demeanor.

He has a tendency to laugh after everything he says. Even if he says something serious, he'll follow it up with a little awkward laugh or smirk. Almost as if to say, "I got ya" or "top that."

Scuttlebutt has it that he was promoted to major "below the zone." That's a big deal and means he reached field grade officer rank at an earlier age than most officers. Normally, an officer who gets promoted below the zone is on a fast track to general officer. At least that's how it's perceived.

I somehow feel his arrogant attitude is propelled by this early promotion. He comes across as thinking he better than everyone else. And, I would be OK with that if I could see some action to back it up. All I've seen so far is a guy making "hot air" promises; all show - no go.

As for his "best guy" Capt Kendall ... well to start he's an Air Force Academy grad but I never would have picked him as one. He just doesn't seem to have any military bearing. He comes across to me like a guy who just put away his surfboard and then threw on a military uniform cause it looks cool.

He looks and acts like a surfer dude. He's got blond hair and blue eyes and the girls all flock to him. But, it seems, once he starts talking to them they drift away. He's not a good conversationalist; I find it difficult and awkward to engage in even short dialogs with him.

His lives in the single officer flats so I see him from time to time and bump into him every once in a while. But, we are not compatible. I get the most uncomfortable feeling when I'm around him. He's seems to be the master of bad news. "Oh, that won't work! That's dumb. I've tried that before, it's a waste of time. That's no fun." Along with a host of other under-whelming statements.

I remember wearing my brother's West Point jacket outside the officers flat one day and Stan had to share his wisdom. He was up on the balcony looking down and there were about 5 or 6 other officers mulling around.

"Hey Sean, we used to make fun of Academy alumni who still wear their cadet uniforms. We'd call them Dweebs. Ha Ha!" He stated in his deadpan, unfunny, insecure manner.

The other officers hanging around smirked but I didn't feel any need to defend myself as Stan's manner was so awkward. I felt resentment but I also felt bad for him as he seemed to alienate just about everyone.

And, this was Maj Monroe's "Best Software Guy?" Oh boy!

I interjected as they both took a breath to start launching more excuses. "Why didn't you guys bring this up months ago when we started? Why did you continue to tell me it wouldn't be a problem? What's changed?"

Maj Monroe fired a salvo, essentially ignoring my questions, "Where's the requirement for this test? Show me where we have a requirement to complete this TRW all commands test?"

I knew we were in trouble now as he's trying to change the rules of engagement. He knows the TRW guys will never back down. But, he thinks he can win by making an end run; use requirements and regulations to wear down your opponent. After all, if we can't show a requirement, the software guys can claim victory – "You're asking us to commit manpower and resources to a task we're not required to do!"

In other words – "GOTCHA!"

I finally got them out of my office when I said, "I'll talk to the DO and the TRW guys."

I called the DO, "Sir, the software guys say they can't do the test. They can't get the new simulator working."

Maj Reed was perplexed and upset, "What do you mean they can't do it? I thought they said they'd have it done this week? Didn't Maj Monroe tell us he had his best guy on it and not to worry?"

"Well, it turns out his best guy can't do it. And, the problem is this; the TRW guys won't authorize any commands to the new spacecraft until the All Commands Test is successfully completed. They insist all the commands need to be verified on the ground – via the new simulator – first." I explained.

Maj Reed shot back, "That puts us in a big bind. This test could be the difference between accepting the new satellite and telling headquarters the ground station is not ready. How embarrassing would that be? We've got to get this test completed. Sean, I want you to set up a meeting for tomorrow. Make sure the software and TRW guys are there. Let's meet right after the morning meeting to sort it out first thing."

Software: "Show me the requirement?"
18 Dec 1990 Tuesday

This morning, right after the morning meeting, the TRW and software guys stayed behind to discuss the "all commands test" issue. The TRW guys were Jack Dubois and Steve Lingham; from software it was Maj Monroe and his "best guy" Capt Kendall. And finally, myself and Maj Reed.

Steve Lingham is the TRW site manager.

The meeting became animated very quickly with both sides digging in. The DO and I tried to keep the discussion rational and on focus. But, emotions started taking over.

"Show me the requirement for this test? Show me where it says we have to complete this test before accepting the new satellite?" Maj Monroe questioned with a low calm voice but with a dash of contempt.

Then after a bit of silence he followed up his position almost like a lawyer who knows he's going to win the case, "You show me the requirement and I'll get it done. But, if there's no requirement, then why should I waste my precious manpower on a task that doesn't need to be done."

The TRW guys were not going to give ground. They knew how ridiculous this sounded especially after Maj Monroe had boasted about how he didn't need any help from outside agencies and his guys could get it done. And, his constant battle cry, "Don't worry."

Jack Dubois spoke up first, "Why are you asking for a requirement now? Why didn't you ask when we first started getting prepared for the new spacecraft? Why bring up this objection now when we're going to get the satellite in a little over a week?

Maj Monroe dug in his heels, "Look, you show me a requirement and I'll do it. It's that simple."

"You're kidding right? You stood up at every single GSR meeting and told the site you could do the test and now you're backing out?" Jack shot back.

Maj Monroe then let out the truth. "I had my best guy, Capt Kendall, on the job last week for 60 hours. If he can't do it, it can't be done. Isn't there another way we can verify the commands? Can't we just print out the commands and then compare them manually against what's in the documentation?"

His best guy couldn't do it, so now he's trying to wiggle out of it. He's backtracking and looking for a compromise; looking for a way out.

Jack didn't want any part of it. "Manually comparing the database is a bogus check. What if there's a typo in the docs? We know the documentation is always done last when the budget is depleted and is usually thrown together in a hurry. Besides, it would take weeks to make such a manual comparison. I won't accept that as a valid test. The only way to verify the spacecraft command data base is by running the all commands test. It must be done. They did it back in Denver, why can't we do it here?"

Maj Monroe played his trump card again, "Show me the requirement."

Maj Reed could see the conversation was going nowhere. He called an end to the meeting.

Afterwards Jack spoke to me. He was visibly upset and gave me some stern words, "How can you be so passive? Those guys kept telling you for months that they could do it and now they come back asking for 'requirements.' If we don't get this test done, you're not going to be able to command this new spacecraft. We're going to look pretty silly sitting out here in the desert twiddling our thumbs while the new spacecraft hovers over our ground station. Sean, you gotta get those guys to complete that test. All they gotta do is ask the guys in Denver for some help and we're there. I don't know why they're so afraid to ask for help"

I listened alertly and started feeling dejected. His words stung because they struck too close to the bone; too close to the truth. I started feeling like I played an active role in this disaster by not pressing the software guys earlier for results. Why didn't I call Denver? Why didn't I start playing around with the new simulator; seeing if I could get it to run? Why didn't I call for assistance when the software guys kept dragging their heels; not showing us any progress? All they gave me was lip service and I accepted it. I feel low.

My strategy didn't work. I felt it was their task. They accepted it right from the start. If they felt they couldn't do it all they had to do was say so. But, instead Maj Monroe kept assuring me it was alright; his team could do it; don't worry.

For me to step in and take an active role in his action item is not my style. I don't believe in telling someone how to do their job. Especially if they know what they're doing; if they are professional and they know their stuff. But, I guess that's the catch here ... apparently, Maj Monroe and his team don't know what they're doing and are not willing to admit it and therefore tried to bluff their way through. Now the game is up and it's reached a crescendo. My role as the GSR lead was to make sure nothing like this happened.

I failed.

"I want you to complete the all commands test"

19 Dec 1990 Wednesday

I walked onto the ops floor this morning and saw Maj Reed, Jack and Maj Monroe involved in a heated discussion.

I heard Maj Monroe complaining in the DO's ear. "Sir, there's no requirement to do the test. TRW knows it. They're making a big stink cause they want the test done. They're threatening you about not being able to command the new spacecraft but it's a bluff. They'll come around."

Jack then jumped in asking, "Maj Reed, are you willing to accept responsibility for any bad commands getting sent to the spacecraft? How are you going to explain a bad command going up when you didn't test the commands first on the ground through the simulator?"

Maj Reed had a look of extreme frustration. He was stuck. He wanted out of this mess.

After a few more minutes of useless dialog, Jack and Maj Monroe walked off the ops floor. I'd been watching from a few feet away. I turned to go back to my office when I heard Maj Reed say, "Sean, come here."

What he said next shocked me. I wasn't prepared. I was totally caught off guard when Maj Reed said, "Sean, I want you to complete the all commands test."

He asked in such a casual manner; as if he wanted me to get him some lunch from the chow hall? No big deal. Just do it.

My first response was silence followed by a big "GULP!" I was stunned. I don't know anything about the simulator. Why are you asking me to do it?

It reminded me of the time when I was a medic at Mather AFB Sacramento California. We were in the emergency room. The doctors were working on a heart attack patient and they couldn't get the probe into his heart to shock it back to life. After three doctors took their best shot at poking the probe into the patient, Dr Benson turned to me and said, "Hey Sean, wanna try?"

It was at this juncture that I knew the patient was gone. The game was over and this was the doctor's way of letting off steam; doctor's humor, I suppose. I didn't think it was too funny although I did put on a little smirk as I replied, "I don't think so Doc."

Well, now Maj Reed was turning to me – the low ranking most inexperience guy – and asking me to save the patient; get it breathing; bring it back to life. Only this patient is the new spacecraft simulator that seems to be – very much – dead.

As I looked at the DO, I could see he was at the end of his rope. He had nowhere else to turn. Things had gotten so bad he's resorted to asking me to complete the task.

I couldn't let him down. What was I going to say, "No?"

The DO wasn't looking for me to wiggle out of it. I knew he wanted it done; he didn't care how; just get it done. I felt like I was given a task I was wholly unqualified for; but I also felt that I could still give it a good try; I could at least find out what's going on; I could get to the bottom of the mystery.

Finally, after what seemed like a long pause and a bit of staring, I came out of it and responded the only way that seemed reasonable. I looked at the DO and uttered two words - "Yes, sir."

I left the ops floor and started walking to the cafeteria for a cup of coffee; to get thinking about what to do next. My total focus turned to getting a solution. I had my antenna up. I was now in the hunt; the hunt to discover the secret of getting this new simulator up and breathing.

Little did I know, my decision to get a cup of coffee saved my bacon. As I started down the main operations area hallway, I saw Brad Allen come out of the Satellite Readout Station (SRS) work center door and start heading towards me. Apparently he was on his way to the ops floor. My mind was focused on my three highest priority tasks – 1) get the new simulator running; 2) get the new simulator running; 3) get the new simulator running.

"Hello Brad." I said as I took a brief moment away from my focus.

"G'day Sean," came the cheerful response from Aussie Brad.

I have a good relationship with Brad. He is a good guy to have on your team if you need hardware assistance. He's been around for years and is one of the site "go-to" guys.

Brad is a crusty old salt. He sports a scruffy light reddish beard; looks like he could use a couple of good meals to get some meat on his bones; has a bit of a jittery way about him that says, "get to the point – don't waste my time." He's very well respected at site and you don't want to mess with him. But, when you need help, you call Brad.

Well, it turns out these sort of thoughts about Brad must have flashed through my mind as we passed in the hallway, because I suddenly stopped, looked back and yelled, "Hey Brad! Can I talk to you for a minute?"

This was a long shot. I didn't think Brad could help me at all. But, my focus – my subconscious mind – said, "ASK HIM!"

"What'ya need Sean?"

"Brad, I'm in a real bind. I'm not sure if this is your area but I gotta ask ya"

"No worries Sean, what is it?" I got Brad curious but I really didn't think the conversation would go very far. A few sentences; a few blank stares and I'd be back on my way down the hallway for my cup of coffee.

"Well, I'm just wondering, do you know anything about how to operate the new spacecraft simulator?" I thought I'd just go for the whole enchilada; ask him the big question. His response shocked me.

"Yeah, I know how to operate it. We had to use it to test our new hardware. The only way to check out the new equipment is with this new simulator. It's a pain in the ass (arse), but we got it working."

I almost fell over. How could I go from the software guys who say it's impossible to the hardware guys who say, "No worries?" Doesn't make any sense.

"Brad, the software guys had their best guy on the job all last week and he couldn't get it working – why's that?" I questioned him in a most disbelieving tone.

"That's cause their best guy doesn't know what he's doing!" Brad, shot back like a rifle.

"If you hardware guys know how to operate it, then why didn't you show him how?"

"Because he never asked us! The software guys know we can operate the damn thing but they were too stubborn and proud to ask for any help. They just stay on the other side of the hallway locked in their area and don't want anything to do with us. If they had asked, we would have been glad to show them what we know. But, they paraded around like know-it-alls and blew us off."

"So, you guys can run the spacecraft commands through the simulator?"

"No, what we can do is get it up and running. You need to get the TRW guys to run the test from the ops room." Brad, replied showing great confidence. I was getting excited but still a bit skeptical.

"Alright, let me get this straight ... You can get the simulator up and running; hold it up in the air while we run the commands through it from the ops area – is that right?" I stood there with my hands in the air as if I was holding up an imaginary simulator.

"You got it. We can get the beast up and running and then you guys run your test. It's that simple." Brad now had me convinced.

"Brad, if I can get the guys organized this morning to run the test, can you and your boys get the simulator up and running this morning or is that too quick?

"We can do that. Just give us about a half hour for the setup and we'll be ready."

"Thanks Brad. I'll get back with you shortly."

As I walked away heading towards the cafeteria, my mind started working overtime. Who can I talk to about running the test? The TRW guys have been essentially out of the loop; they've just been waiting for the test to be completed; they haven't really been involved so I didn't think they were the right people to talk to.

So, I took my hot cup of coffee and headed back to the ops floor to look for clues; inspiration; ideas.

As I entered the ops floor I saw TSgt Hollings one of our best Ground Station Operators (GSO).

"Hey, Sgt Hollings, the hardware guys know how to get the new simulator up and running, now I just need someone to run the all commands test," I floated my problem out to the seasoned GSO and career Technical Sergeant (TSgt). I'm sure glad I did. It was almost as if divine intervention was leading me to the answers.

"We've been working with the IBM guys. They're down here for some other work but they are experts with the new spacecraft simulator. They could run your test – no problem," he confidently told me; almost in the same manner you'd tell someone where the latrine is located. No big deal; just housekeeping stuff.

It turns out I know one of the IBM guys. I used to work with him in Denver when he was in the Air Force. Now, he is a high paid IBM engineer fixing and/or installing software and hardware. I have seen him a couple of times on site and say hello but I had no idea he would be my go-to man for the new simulator ... until TSgt Hollings told me!

I immediately started walking very quickly to the IBM work area.

"Hi Jim, I'm told that you're pretty handy with the new spacecraft simulator ...?"

"Yeah, I work with it a lot. It's got a lot of capabilities but it's not very user friendly," replied Jim, my new-found spacecraft simulator expert.

"I'm wondering if you'd do me a favor. You see I'm in kind of a bind. I gotta get this all commands test completed before the new spacecraft gets here on station in a little over a week. Otherwise the TRW guys won't authorize any commands. So, can you provide some guidance or oversight or just some general help in getting it completed?"

Jim's reply was straight from Heaven! I wanted to kiss him.

"Sean, just give me the test procedure and we'll run it for you. We'll work with the hardware guys and have it done in no time. When do you want it done?"

I couldn't believe what I was hearing. "When do I want it done?" I felt like I was ordering French fries from McDonalds. Is it that easy? If it's that easy why can't the software guys do it? And, even if it's difficult, why didn't the software guys just asks the experts for help? Why didn't they take advantage of the IBM expertise that's right here?

At this stage, all that didn't matter. What mattered now was crossing the finish line. Let's get this party started and get the all commands test done.

"Well, if we could get it done this morning that would be great."

"Ok, I'll head down to the ops floor in fifteen minutes and get everything set up. We'll look at starting the test in about an hour. Once we get everything set up it shouldn't take very long to complete the test," Jim relayed his plan as confidently as if he told me he could drive to the store and buy a gallon of milk.

I walked onto the ops floor and saw Jim, TSgt Hollings, other IBM reps, Jack and other TRW reps and military guys hovering around the GSO work area computer. I'd gotten permission from the crew commander to use the offline computer to run our test. I had no issue getting the crew commander's permission as the DO made completion of the all commands test a top priority.

I stood back and watched them setup. I watched in amazement as they coordinated the test with Brad and the guys back in the satellite readout station work area – the hardware department. They worked like a well-oiled machine. I could tell they'd done the set-up many times before. Yes, it was cumbersome but they proceeded through all the mundane steps like clockwork and in a businesslike fashion.

After a short while, I left the ops floor and ducked back in to my office. I felt like my presence was not a force for good. Instead it had a two-fold negative effect. First, it gave the impression of impatience. "Hurry up and get this done! I'm waiting! What's taking so long?" Next, it gave the impression that I didn't have confidence in them. For these two reasons I made the very short walk to my office and closed the door leaving them to work their magic.

I sat down at my desk and got to work on another project. I think it was only about a half hour later when my office door burst open and I heard the sweet sound of TSgt Hollings's voice, "Lt Mitchell, the test is completed. All commands have been sent to the new simulator and verified. The TRW guys are happy with the results and have signed off on the successful completion of the test."

I was floored. I was in a state of disbelief. I walked out to the ops floor and talked to the IBM and TRW guys. They were all in a very good mood; lots of banter going back and forth.

"Sean, the test went without a hitch. The hardware guys and IBM guys got the simulator up and running and then they just ran the commands through in no time. All commands checked out. We've signed off on the test. We're OK to send commands to the new spacecraft," Jack confirmed the great news.

I then jumped back into my office to make the phone call. I couldn't believe I was about relay the incredible news.

After all, just this morning we were in despair – the completion of the all commands test seemed almost impossible – a show stopper – a big embarrassment for the site. I thought we'd be calling Headquarters asking for help ... and that looks bad – very bad. As if we can't solve our own site problems. And, how would we explain why we waited so long? How would I explain that it took this long to discover we had a problem? I am the GSR coordinator; I would foot a lot of the blame; and I might add, rightfully so.

As I picked up the phone I couldn't stop my hand from shaking. I was surprised as I watched my hand shake; I could see it but I was powerless to stop it. I almost didn't even care; it was a sign of how excited I was; how happy; how relieved. I was shaking from happiness. If you're going to shake, let it be because you're happy!

My shaking finger hit the speed dial for the DO. I could hear him pick up on the other end and give me his standard greeting, "Reed here."

Another lucky sign ... seven times out of ten the DO is not in his office. It's not easy to catch him at his desk. But, this morning, I did. All the planets seemed to be lining up today.

I was shaking but I put on my best newscaster voice as I relayed the unbelievable news, "Sir, Lt Mitchell here. Just wanted to let you know the all commands test has been completed successfully. All spacecraft commands for the new satellite have been run through the new simulator. All commands have been checked out and verified."

I waited impatiently for his response. I wanted it to be a good one and he didn't let me down. His most eloquent response was music to my ears ...

"You're kidding?"

"No sir. It's done. The TRW guys have signed off on it and we're all set to start commanding the new spacecraft when it arrives."

"How on earth did you do it? The software guys couldn't do it and they were working on it for months. And, now you tell me you got in done this morning – that's crazy!" He blurted.

I was hoping he'd ask.

"Well sir, I didn't do it. I just talked to the hardware guys and then found some IBMers who just happen to be on site - and just happen to be experts on the new spacecraft simulator – and asked them to do it. Once we had the right guys on the job, it was a cinch!"

"Good work Sean. What a relief. The TRW guys wouldn't budge and the software guys were digging their heels in too. We were in a real bind. Thanks for fixing this mess," he told me in an excited rapid-fire voice.

With my shaking hand, I hung up the phone. One of the most satisfying phone calls I ever made.

Letter of Congratulations

21 Dec 1990 Friday

The software department is at war with me. I'm no longer welcome there. I'm public enemy number one.

Why?

Because I wrote a letter of congratulations to all the people who contributed to the successful completion of the all commands test.

I praised Brad and the hardware department; Jim and the visiting IBM team; TSgt Hollings.

I didn't mention any TRW guys because they didn't really do anything; they just observed. And, I also didn't mention – and this is where I got in trouble – the software department.

Essentially, the congratulatory letter smears the software department something ferocious. As I wrote the letter I kind of sensed this would happen but I wasn't going to let that stop me from writing it.

The letter basically says this ... the hardware department, the IBM visitors and one of our own GSOs saved us from impending disaster. They completed a critical ground station readiness test; one that had to be completed prior to accepting the new spacecraft.

Just about everyone on site knows the software department has been assigned this task. Just about everyone knows they couldn't do it. Just about everyone knows they tried to get out of it at the last moment.

And now, the hardware department, a few site IBM visitors and a local GSO completed the test easily in about two hours.

It doesn't look good for the software department. They're livid.

My question to the software department is this ... why didn't you just ask for some help? Why didn't you talk to people who already knew how to operate the new simulator? Why start from scratch? Why not focus on getting a successful result instead of worrying about who gets the credit?

I'm sorry the software department is so upset. But, I'm not sorry about writing the congratulations letter that is making the rounds at site, up to Headquarters and to IBM in Boulder.

The software department could have been part of the congratulations letter but they chose to be non-team players; wanting all the glory for themselves. Instead they get all the blame.

FLT 15 Comes into View

26 Dec 1990 Wednesday (Boxing Day)

Today our ground antennas picked up the signal from Flight 15 for short periods of time then it would drop out. The satellite is at the very edge of our Eastward viewing. Our antennas are looking out towards the Pacific Ocean to pick it up.

This is sooner than I expected. I asked the antenna guys in the SRS about the elevation angles – "They're negative!" – came back the reply. This means we're picking up the signal "in the dirt." Our ground antennas are essentially looking downward to see the new satellite. The people who setup Woomera were pretty smart because our antennas look eastward through low lying terrain along the geosync satellite corridor; along the equator. Good thinking.

I took a walk outside with the SRS guys and we verified this. When you look in a north eastward direction the terrain is flat as a pancake.

Lt Kelly Decertified – Again

31 Dec 1990 Monday

When I came into work this morning I got hit with the bad news. Last Friday, the best crew commander on site – Australian Navy Lt

Ethan Kelly – got decertified. They escorted him and his deputy out of the SOC. That's his second time since I've been here. I thought there had to be something wrong; some mistake. And I was right. He's our most knowledgeable and experienced crew commander; it doesn't make sense that he would get decertified.

I discovered this situation is similar to the last one; Lt Kelly had to make a choice – do the right thing or do the safe thing and follow headquarters procedures. He chose to do the right thing. Now he's in trouble.

Ethan has been at site for almost four years. The Australians have a much longer tour than us Yanks. Ethan is even more of an exception because the normal tour length is three years but he's extended for another year.

The US crew commanders are in and out. Normal tour is 15 months if you're single or come down alone; 24 months if you bring your family. And, most of the Yanks leave after one tour. It's not good for your career as an officer to stay down here at site too long. Apparently, the Air Force looks at it as "homesteading" and they feel your growth as an officer is stunted if you stay in one location too long.

Most Aussie's laugh at this logic. They feel it's ridiculous to pull someone away from an assignment just when they're starting to get good at their job. And, it's about the two year point where the crew commanders start to get really confident at their job. And, just when they're getting good – they leave.

Well, Lt Kelly is good. He's "the man." The guys all look up to him. He's got the swagger and it's backed up by his talent. He's put in the work, he's done the study, he's passed the tests – the real ones on the ops floor where it counts – he's a pro. The crew members know it; the other crew commanders know it. It's not because he's been here the longest – although that helps because he's seen a lot and experienced a lot – but it's more because he's worked at being his best at the job. He's put in the study, he's seen more real launches, and he's seen more training tapes, studied more of the tech books, and learned a lot of the tricks from the contractor satellite engineers.

Well, now he's decertified ... again.

Here's the story as told to me ...

Ethan heard the yell from one of his crew members, "Stand by!"

"When you get it built send it up," he instructed the crew member.

"Comin at ya sir!" The crew member sent it up for review.

Ethan knew straight away it was a valid launch. He didn't need to look at the launch numbers displayed on the computer screen; he could tell just from the "dots" on the screen. He'd seen it before; he'd seen both real launches and training tapes showing this same signature. No doubt – it was a valid launch. He'd already made the decision to send it high speed.

And, it was an important launch – coming out of Iraq. It turns out it was another one of Saddam's SCUD test launches. Yes, it's a small IRBM, but with all the saber rattling going on, our ability to catch these smaller missiles is getting a much higher profile. The more of these he fires the better we're going to get at detecting and reporting them.

Once the missile is detected, Ethan's got a two minute window in which to release the high speed message. After that, it's considered late; automatic decertification.

As Ethan considered his options – making sure of his decision - his deputy, Capt Henry Manning, chimed in with a warning, "We haven't got all the criteria for high speed. The TAI's too low; there's not enough motion; we can't send it high speed."

Ethan knew Henry was right. But, he also knew it was a valid launch. To send it low speed would be criminal. Sending low speed would be the safe way to go; can't get decertified that way. But, he'd feel bad for doing it. It would be like seeing someone drowning and instead of getting out and helping you drive off and make a phone call to 911 or 000. You've done your part; but that person will probably drown because help came too late. You'd feel guilty about it for the rest of your life.

Ethan started thinking ... he was looking for a way to justify his decision to send it high speed. He was running out of time.

Then it came to him. Of course - The new satellite! It wasn't operational but it was on-line and probably saw the same event. The crews had it set up for "hot shadow" so it's processing the mission just the same as the on-line system.

"Hey, do you have a report from the new bird?" Ethan called down to the crew.

"Yes sir, it's got a better angle."

"Let me have a look."

"Ah ha! There's your motion mate. Flight 15 is showing all the motion we need to confirm a valid launch. Send that bad boy!"

Ethan was demonstrating – yet again - why he is "THE MAN." He's writing his name in the record books – greatest crew commander ever.

That is until HQ got a hold of him.

On Saturday, HQ sent a message to the DO calling for Lt Kelly to be decertified.

Yes it was a valid launch. But, the on-line computer did not show enough motion for sending the message out high speed.

Yes, the off-line computer, with non-operational satellite data, did show enough motion but HQ ruled you can't use a non-operational asset to make an operational assessment.

This is nuts.

They escorted Lt Kelly and Capt Manning out of the SOC and unceremoniously decertified them in front of their crew and the contractors.

Yes, Ethan got decertified but this event only serves to enhance his reputation as a hero even more with everyone here at site. He performed masterfully. He performed above and beyond expectations. He used his creative thinking to find a way to justify sending out a "borderline" missile launch via the high speed network. The crew knew what he'd done; they knew he was in the right. Who cares if HQ didn't see it that way – this guy is the real deal; he's got the right stuff.

We need more guys like Ethan in the ranks.

Ohio State Loses to Air Force.
3 Jan 1991 Thursday

I was visiting the guys on the ops floor today and they were talking about college football. I haven't been keeping up with it so I didn't even know the bowl games were being played. And, I wish I could have kept it that way.

I'm a 1987 Ohio State grad and I found out shortly after arriving on campus that football – at Ohio State – means one thing; and one thing only. And, that one thing is this ... EVERYTHING!

I remember my last year at Ohio State in the fall quarter of 1986. The football team lost the first two games of the season; two losses in a row to start the season. The last time that happened was in the 1800s!

I was amazed at how these two losses made the mood on campus so somber. The professors gave more homework and graded more harshly; the students seemed so dejected – as if they just found out there's really no Santa Clause.

The mood was so low, I was almost expecting to hear a campus-wide announcement, "Sorry but we're closing down the university. There's really no point in continuing with the academic year if the football team can't win."

When I graduated, I thought I'd have to swear allegiance to Ohio State football in exchange for my diploma.

Ohio State football is serious business.

I remember football Saturday afternoons at my apartment in Columbus and all you could hear is the distant sound of radios and televisions tuned to the Ohio State game. Everything else was quiet; no road noise; nobody out playing tennis; no kids on the swings ... just the breeze; like a ghost town. Then the silence would be broken by loud screaming, whooping, and/or crying either for joy, sadness or anger depending on whether or not the play went for or against Ohio State.

So, when one of the crew yelled out, "How bout those Buckeyes Lt Mitchell?" I got nervous. I was hoping for good news, that way I knew the campus would be safe for another academic year.

"Did they win?" I asked, and then mentally ducked to brace myself for the worst.

The crew member was hoping I'd ask. He wound up and hit me with the painful truth, "They lost to Air Force!" He followed up his line with a big bountiful laugh. His laughter was contagious and next thing all the crew guys are laughing and watching the red embarrassment line on my body climb up my neck and then completely cover my face.

How could Ohio State lose to Air Force? Ohio State has a 50 pound per man weight advantage at the line of scrimmage over Air Force. All they have to do is bounce the Air Force front line out of the way and then even I could run the ball through the gaping hole!

This must be a new low point for the football program.

I wonder if Ohio State will close down.

DIY Air Con Repairs

7 Jan 1991 Monday.

I had an interesting, informative and disheartening chat with my next door neighbor Sgt Newtown this evening. He greeted me in a way that said, "I got to get something off my chest."

"Hello Lieutenant." He stated as he walked straight over to me.

"Can I talk to you?" He asked. I was surprised and curious.

Sgt Newtown is a good troop. I like him. He's very personable. We've chatted across our common fence line from time to time.

He's a skinny guy with dirty blonde hair and a face smooth as a 12 year old. He looks like he just walked off a dairy farm in Nebraska.

He's stationed down here with his beautiful Korean wife and lovely newborn baby.

"Sure, what's on your mind? I replied observing his most serious expression.

"Well, I'm in a tough spot and if something doesn't happen soon, I'm going to have to take some action."

"Oh yeah, what's the trouble?" I replied and then got a story that makes you wonder how the military stays open for business.

Here's a recap of what he told me ...

The air conditioner in his house broke last Tuesday. He's been without any air con for over five days. In Woomera - in the middle of summer – that's a serious issue. In his case it's even more serious because he has a newborn baby.

Temperatures have been hitting 40 Celsius; that's over 100 Fahrenheit. You can't last in the sun very long; you've got to find some shade. Also, its stays hot all night. Without aircon is very hard to sleep in this heat.

He had to wait until last Wednesday to call housing because Tuesday was a holiday; New Years. Housing finally sent a maintenance man to fix the problem on Friday morning. It didn't take long for the maintenance guy to figure out the air con unit needs a new motor; he ordered a replacement.

Sgt Newtown called over to housing on Friday afternoon and asked how long it would take to get the new motor. Housing told him, "We don't know, but we have 15 days to get the part in, after that it's considered late. But, it's no use bothering us before then because by regulation we have 15 days."

YANKS IN THE OUTBACK

Since the air conditioner broke, Sgt Newtown, his wife and new born daughter have been sleeping downstairs. It's way too hot to sleep upstairs. And, he told me during the daytime it's too hot for his wife and baby even downstairs. They have to go to a neighbor's house or the library to find aircon and stay cool.

Today, after a weekend of sweltering heat, he called housing again to plead his case, "I've got a newborn daughter in the house; she can't take this heat. Is there any way we can speed up the process? Or, can we move to a new house while waiting for the part to come in?"

Housing was not impressed, "Don't call again. We've ordered the part. When it comes in we'll send someone out to install it. If we don't fix it in 15 days, then you can call."

Sgt Newtown found himself in a serious bind – so he got creative. He had an idea. There's a vacant townhouse a few doors down; he decided to check out the air-conditioning unit to see if it looked ok. Maybe he could he just cannibalize the unit; swap his bad part for the good one in the other house? He inspected the other air-conditioning unit and discovered his plan was workable. The chances were very good that a parts swap would work.

So, he called housing again, "Hey, why can't we swap parts with air-conditioning unit in the vacant house on my block? Then when the new part comes in just put it in the vacant house air-conditioning unit. That would solve the problem."

Housing wouldn't hear of it, "We can't do that. We can't make a working unit defective – it's against regulations. You'll just have to wait until the part comes in and we send someone out to install it."

I couldn't believe what I was hearing – Insanity! Makes no sense!

I pictured his family boiling in the house.

I offered for them to stay at my place but he turned me down saying, "We'll be alright. We stay downstairs at night; it's bearable. And my wife and daughter stay with a friend or at the library during the day when I'm at work. But thanks for offering."

DIY Aircon II: Problem Solved!

8 Jan 1991 Tuesday

Sgt Newtown is on top of the world today. He got creative and fixed his air conditioner. He took matters into his own hands.

He knocked on my back door; wanting to share the good news.

"I took the motor from the vacant house and used it in my air conditioner – it worked. I was really just conducting a test. I planned to put the motor back and then call housing to have a maintenance guy come around and install it per their regulations. But, once I had it in there and working I changed my mind. Instead I'll call housing tomorrow and let them know I did it and they can put the replacement motor in the vacant house."

I think Sgt Newton deserves a medal. He took the initiative. He solved the problem. Instead of complaining about it, he took appropriate action to fix it.

I congratulated him and then expressed my doubts about his plan to notify housing, "Are you sure you want let housing know what you did?

He shamed me a bit with his explanation.

"I want to do the right thing. It wouldn't be right not to tell them. That would make it look like I'm hiding something. I'm not hiding anything. Besides, they were going to swap the motors anyway; I just did it for them."

I told you Sgt Newtown is a great guy!

GSR Meeting: All good; we're on the bird all the time

9 Jan 1991 Wednesday

We had another GSR meeting today. We don't really need it but I think the guys wanted to have one out of habit and to just share any news.

Everyone gathered in the commander's conference room and the mood was upbeat. We've been tracking the new bird since late December. We've had no issues processing telemetry with our ground equipment and we've even been processing mission data with our offline computer system.

We're ready to take the bird now.

But, that's not how it works. It's still going through its headquarters checkout phase. We get the bird when headquarters says we can have it.

Right now the plan is for HQ to continue their checkout while the bird drifts to its target sub-point of 105 degrees E longitude. This is essentially right over Singapore. So, we're calling the new satellite our Singapore bird. Once it reaches Singapore, we take it. HQ tells us this will be in late January.

DIY Aircon III: No Good Deed Goes Unpunished

12 Jan 1991 Saturday

I thought Sgt Newtown's aircon story was over and concluded with a happy ending.

Not even close.

I saw him this morning after he returned home from working a mid-shift. He looked even more dejected than when his air con wasn't working.

What happened? How could things be worse now?

Sgt Newtown made a fatal mistake. He called housing.

He called housing to tell them the good news, "I swapped the motors myself and now my air conditioner is working. When the new motor comes in just install it in the other air conditioner at the vacant house."

Did housing congratulate him for his stellar achievement? Did they write him up for an award? Did they cite him for taking clever initiative; for rescuing his wife and newborn daughter from the extreme heat?

No.

Again – not even close.

The reaction from housing was stunningly absurd; even absurd by government and military standards ...

"What you did is illegal. You cannot do that, it's against the law. We can bring charges up against you. We're going to report you to Civil Engineering. You are in big trouble."

Yesterday, Sgt Newtown got called in to see the Chief of Civil Engineering, Maj Kevin Spence. I like Maj Spence but his response was nothing short of bizarre; nothing short of ridiculous; nothing short of stupid.

To me this situation represented an opportunity for Maj Spence to shine; to show massive amounts of wisdom; massive amounts of compassion; massive amounts of common sense.

But no – That's not what happened.

Instead Kevin took the road to stupidity. He rallied the troops and charged headlong over the cliff of ignorance.

Here's how Maj Spense chose to open the conversation, "Sgt Newtown, you have the right to remain silent. Anything you say can and will be used against you in a court of law."

Brilliant opening.

He continued his ride off the cliff of common sense into the valley of the vapid; the depths of the dull-witted; the depression of the dense.

Do you realize you broke the law? Do you realize I can have you locked up?"

Sgt Newtown just sat there trying to understand how the response to his actions could be so ridiculous; so opposite from what common sense would dictate.

Maj Spence continued his dopey diatribe, "Do you have an electrician license? Did you have any authorization from housing to be on the other property? I can get you on removing and installing electrical equipment without a license and on two counts of burglary - one for taking the motor out of your house and one for taking the motor out of the other house.

"I'm going to be lenient on you this time because you're a good troop and you don't have a history of misbehavior. So, instead of turning you over to the legal guys and courts martial, I'm going give you an article 15."

Maj Spence thought he was being generous.

No way.

An article 15 is "non-judicial punishment." It's the military way of meting out its own special form of justice. Essentially, once you get hit with an article 15, your career is ruined. Good luck trying to get promoted with an article 15 on your record.

So, Sgt Newtown's enterprising solution for fixing his broken air conditioner was rewarded with a virtual career ending punishment.

I wish this story ended another way. I wish it ended with Maj Spence as the hero instead of the villain. I wish Maj Spence was more concerned with the welfare of his troops instead of the welfare of his career. I wish I could report that Maj Spence tore through the reams of red tape to arrive at a solution that reflected great wisdom instead of great folly.

But, I can't.

And, unfortunately, this same story – in different forms – probably goes on nearly every day in the military and the government in general.

Yes, I agree, it's sad.

What could Maj Spence have done differently? What would I have liked to see him do?

Well, glad you asked.

First, I would love to have told you Maj Spence nipped this problem in the bud. Right up front he could have kicked it in the guts and fixed it quickly.

Let's ask a few pointed questions to get things rolling on just how he could have approached this situation.

What if Maj Spence's air-conditioning unit broke in his house; how long do you think it would take before it was up and running again?

Do you think Housing would have told their boss, Maj Spence, to sit tight for 15 days in the searing heat?

Or do you think housing would have come up with a more creative response; a response that fixed the problem; a response that fixed the problem fast?

If the problem had been with Maj Spence's air conditioner, I'll bet it would have been fixed in one day – maybe sooner.

That's just my guess.

What could good old Maj Spence have done to help Sgt Newtown?

Well here are a few ideas ...

1. Tell the Chief of Housing to get Sgt Newtown's air-conditioner working – now! If someone has to wait 15 days for a part it will be the chief of housing not Sgt Newtown.

2. When Sgt Newtown suggested a parts swap with the vacant unit, this idea should have been pursued with vigor. Get the maintenance guys on it – now!

3. When Sgt Newtown reported his parts swap to housing, Maj Spence could have congratulated him and punished his housing personnel for not supporting this excellent idea.

I would have much preferred to tell a hero story about Maj Spence. That would mean someone in leadership cared; someone took correct action even if that action didn't follow regulations. Someone in leadership had guts and courage.

But, sorry to say, this is another story about an enterprising troop who found a way around the bureaucratic red tape and nonsense to arrive at a clever and creative solution; and then finally, instead of getting a much deserved promotion, he gets an unjust punishment.

Welcome to the military.

Desert Storm Begins: Air War
17 Jan 1991 Thursday

Crazy scene today on the ops floor. The war has begun.

The US is bombing the hell out of Iraq and Kuwait.

It seemed like every five minutes or so, Sgt Long would enter the ops area and yell out the latest news update from CNN.

Sgt Long is one of our GSOs. His voice pitched higher and almost wanted to crack as he relayed each update. He seemed to relish his new – self-appointed - role. And, he's pretty good at it. We all more or less accepted him as our personal "war updater."

A typical call out would go something like this, "US warplanes just bombed Baghdad; over 100 sorties already; no casualties on our side!"

Then he would run back to the break room to get the next round of war information. We watched him throughout the whole process as the break room is adjacent to the ops floor and clearly visible through the large glass windows. We could see him staring at the television screen. Then he'd turn and start back out through the break room door to broadcast the next update.

"No loss of planes and no loss of pilots. That what CNN is reporting about the first raid launched from a base in Saudi; according to a high ranking Saudi official."

SCUD Launch on Israel

18 Jan 1991 Friday

Today I got scared. It happened while walking through the ops support office on my way to the SOC (Satellite Operations Center). I was about four steps from the door when it opened up and Capt Jefferson walked through with a look of terror on his face.

Capt Jefferson is an even keel type of guy. He doesn't get too riled up about things. He's a good officer with a good reputation here at site. His first name is Cornelius but he goes by "Connie." He's black.

I was struck off-guard by his emotional dialog, "Sean, this could be it. This could be the end. This could be the start of World War Three."

"Connie, what are you talking about?" I asked in a low and calm voice. I could see he was distressed and I didn't want to aggravate the situation.

"The Iraqis just launched a SCUD into Israel! The crews saw it plain as day. It's on. This is bad news. This is terrible."

Then he walked past me with a dazed look on his face.

I think I had the same look as I walked into the SOC. But, the crew members had a different reaction.

"Hey Sean, we saw the launch and sent it high speed. We nailed it. CNN just confirmed it; they verified the Iraqis fired a SCUD into Israel," blurted out the on-duty crew commander Capt Trent.

Then he looked past me and shouted out to his crew, "Good work guys! You were all over it! Drinks on me tonight at Spuds!"

Spuds is one of the main crew hangouts spots. It's located right at the turn off point from the main highway into Woomera. Most travelers on the Stuart Highway have heard of Spuds. Spuds is much more popular with travelers than Woomera. Most people won't make the nine kilometer detour to come into Woomera. But, they will pull into Spuds to fill up with petrol, get a hot meal and pour down a few cold beers.

For some reason, the crews prefer Spuds over the other pubs in town. Not sure why, but I hear the crews talking a lot about the latest and greatest parties out at Spuds.

What a contrast – the crew reaction vs Capt Jefferson's reaction to the launch. I guess the crews look at it as doing their job; that's what they're here for; that's their mission. Capt Jefferson is looking at the overall world view; a much scarier perspective.

FLIGHT 15 – We're Taking Operational Control

21 Jan 1991 Tuesday

Received a message today from HQ today saying FLIGHT 15 will arrive at 105 degrees East on or about 31 Jan 1991. When it arrives at 105 we are to take operational control.

This is just a formality as the bird has been fully checked out and signed off by HQ and we have confirmed that we're ready to operate. We've been monitoring the satellite and using it in what's called a "hot shadow" mission configuration. "Hot shadow" is when we set up our second computer string to process mission data but have no high speed reporting capability hooked up. So, if we see a launch on the hot shadow bird, we can't send a high speed warning message.

PART 5: FEB – APR 1991

Letters from the Front

10 Feb 1991 Sunday

Last week I received two letters from the Middle East. One from my younger brother John and one from my cousin Richard.

John is a West Point grad in a deployed tank maintenance battalion from Germany. My Dad says they are deployed to Turkey.

Richard is 19 or 20 years old and with the 2nd Marines 2nd Division about 60 km from the Kuwaiti border. He said the "Air War" doesn't seem to be working to make Hussein give up so the Marines are preparing to make the charge.

Richard had only had six months on his enlistment when he got the bad news about deploying to Saudi Arabia. He doesn't sound like he's too thrilled with the prospect of hand delivering the Iraqi fanatics to the infernal regions. He just wanted to finish his enlistment and get out.

Solid built, good looking kid, good head on his shoulders. I pray the Lord protects him and keeps those Iraqi bullets away from him.

I've been reading the "Weekend Australia" every week since war broke out. The vantage point is very interesting and I'm sure much different from the way the war is portrayed in the US. Most of the articles this week centered on when the ground war is to begin.

I like what the British general Sir Peter has to say – "it's inevitable."

The Americans are still hanging on to the idea that air power can win it. I personally disagree – as Patton said, 'air power cannot take territory or take prisoners!'

The paper said air power may win it but it will take up to six months – much too long for the fragile coalition to hold together. The decision to send in the troops hinges on this – if sending in troops speeds up the victory then the U.S. might have no other option. What they're afraid of are the casualties. One article quoted Dick Chaney (Sec of Defense) as 'wanting to send in the troops at a time when the casualties (Americans) will be minimized.'

The decision to begin the ground war should not lie with the president and certainly not with Mr Cheney (no military background – there should be a law against people serving as Sec of Defense who have no military training – it's like electing a U.S. president who has never lived in the U.S.)

The decision to launch the ground war lies firmly with the military commanders in the field. The president said he was going to let the military fight this one so I hope he keeps good his word!

Gulf War Not Top Story
11 Feb 1991 Monday

Interesting thing about the news tonight – the Gulf War was not the headlines. Top story was the debt of the state bank (South Australia). First time since before the war broke out that it has not been the top and sometimes the only story. Could be we are all beginning to get used to the war.

The Americans are saying the ground war will not begin for another six weeks or so. This after Cheney's and Gen Powell's visit to the front (Saudi). They showed Cheney on the TV saying we're reaching the point of diminishing returns – bombing can only do so much. He's getting the public ready for the inevitable – the ground war. I'll bet they're all just hoping against hope that Hussein will give up. It doesn't look like he will. He seems to thrive off the publicity.

We talked about the war today at work. One of the Aerojet contractors says the bombing campaign is getting to the point where we're just shifting sand – moving the sand dunes back and forth.

Prayer Luncheon – Justifying the War
12 Feb 1991 Tuesday

I attended a prayer luncheon today at the "Oasis Center." The guest speaker was a Royal Australian Air Force Chaplain – a Roman Catholic priest.

He gave a speech – adding a little "fire and brimstone" - about why we are fighting the war in the Middle East, why the allies are "just" in their cause and why we in the military are not warmongers but actually peacekeepers. He cited John F. Kennedy as his inspiration – the words 'bear and burden ... are ringing true today and we are carrying out these words in the middle east today.' He followed a theme along these lines.

He was a good speaker and he was surely convinced of his viewpoint but I was left less than motivated. He seemed to be another "higher up" promoting the party line ... 'We are in the Middle East to promote justice throughout the world ... I trust our leaders judgment, motivations ... leaders like, George Bush and Bob Hawke.'

I'm still not convinced the war is over anything other than oil.

I'll always be suspect of foreign wars and US involvement in them. We have virtually no allies in the Middle East and yet we're parading around like we're best friends with countries like Syria, Egypt, and Saudi Arabia.

This war appears too political for me – very shady – like a lot is going on that we don't know about.

Not Bombing Civilians?
13 Feb 1991 Wednesday

I'm rereading some books on the Vietnam War. I read 40 pages last night – one chapter on Nixon & Kissinger; their dealings in the Vietnam War.

Sad chapter in American history.

I read the chapter because yesterday I got into a discussion with Mr. Jack Dubois (TRW) from work about Vietnam. I claimed the famous Christmas bombings of '72' were a waste of time and that the final agreement signed later was no different than the one refused by the U.S. before the bombings.

Jack wanted to know where I got my information from so I dug up my old book from my history of Vietnam class at Ohio State – book called "America's Longest War." I re-read the chapter and it confirmed what I said about the Christmas bombings – the agreement signed by the US following the bombing had only cosmetic changes to the one rejected by the US prior to the bombings.

The book I'm reading tonight is by a guy named Zinn called "Vietnam: The Logic of Withdrawal" written in '67'. It's very forward thinking. I'm sure he was considered a "commie pinko" in his time. Zinn states in the first chapter "that the claims of statesman & military men to be bombing only military targets should not be taken seriously." This is one of the conclusions he arrived at after serving in WWII as a bombardier in the US Army Air Force.

Ironically, President Bush was on the TV tonight saying that we are not bombing civilian targets in Iraq.

Baghdad Shelter Bombed
14 Feb 1991 Thursday

The Gulf War is about one month old. Today the big news item was the bombing of the shelter in Baghdad. The Iraqis claim it was filled with civilians, US says it was a legitimate military target. The news shows the devastation and the dead bodies and mourning Iraqi people – very sad. Very heart wrenching – just what the Iraqi government wants us to feel. Still, the fact remains – it was our military that did the bombing. Every time we bomb civilian centers we're playing right into the enemy's hand…

I hope and pray that our military leaders are not foolish enough to think that if we bomb the Iraqi people they (the Iraqis) will lose their will to fight and go against Saddam and end the war.

This is a possible outcome but with no historical precedent.

The bombing of civilians usually leads to the forging together of the people against those doing the bombing – the people rally behind their leader. This was true in both England and Germany during WWII. The bombing of London served no other purpose than to further the British will to stand up to Hitler to the last. The bombing of Hamburg rallied the German people around their doomed leader.

YANKS IN THE OUTBACK

Why can't we learn?

The stated United Nations objective is to drive Iraq from Kuwait. Why are we bombing Baghdad? I can see picking off their rocket launchers one by one. I can see cutting off supply lines to Kuwait. I can see sending in the troops to surround Kuwait and then wait for the Iraqi soldiers to come out or just stay put and we'll starve them out.

What I can't see is this quick fix mentality. Bomb everything. When you run out of known military targets start bombing suspected military targets; when you run out of these, bomb civilian targets.

Bomb, Bomb, Bomb. Keep bombing until they give up. I wonder what we're going to do if Saddam doesn't read the script. What if he doesn't give up?

The war is beginning to take on an absurd posture. Are we going to fight or are we going to play around? As far as I'm concerned we've done the bombing necessary and more. It's time to send the soldiers in and take territory (Kuwait) and take prisoners.

The absurd began tonight on the news when the American generals were trying to explain why civilians were bombed. One general explained he was quite satisfied the bunker was a military target. He admitted civilians may have been in the bunker but this is one of Saddam's tactics (to put civilians in military buildings).

He went on to say that some people (Saddam) just don't value human life the way we do. These words just struck me as pathetic; so pious, so moralistic, so patronizing, so believable to the

American public. An American public that desperately wants to believe we are fighting for a just cause. I can almost feel the sentiment ... "Don't let this be another Vietnam. This just can't be another Vietnam."

Well, comments like the general's make me wonder. I can see taking on the Iraqi military but if we are too chicken-shit to take them on then I say we quit bombing the Iraqi civilians and go home.

The mentality of bombing the civilians until the military gives up is ludicrous. The general spoke about people who don't value human life the way we do. I don't consider those who bomb civilians in Baghdad – when the stated war objective is the removal of the enemy from Kuwait – qualified to give moralistic lectures on the value of human life.

Damage Control
15 Feb 1991 Friday

News tonight said Bush is trying to control the damage brought on by the bombing of the bunkers full of civilians. Generals are still trying to explain it. General on TV tonight said they may start telling the Iraqis where they're going to bomb so the civilians can move out.

Informing the Iraqi people where we are going to bomb seems absurd because, if we do, we are in essence admitting the targets are civilian in nature. If the targets are in fact military, then why is any notification needed?

War is simple in nature but also very brutal. Why we try to complicate everything I don't know. Maybe because the government has too big a hand in it. Once the shooting starts the military should take over and the government officials step back.

Bush and Chaney should not be making the decision of when to begin the ground attack – that decision should lie squarely with the field commander. The field commander should demand that authority if he doesn't have it.

Lessons learned ... not learned
17 Feb 1991 Sunday

I'm reading another book on Vietnam called "A Short History of the Vietnam War." The book was edited by my Vietnam history professor from Ohio State, Allan R. Millett. Good professor and good book. Series of articles from the Washington Post newspaper by various authors.

One article that caught my eye, and proved particularly pertinent to the present war is the Middle East, was called "Hard Learned Lessons in a Military Laboratory" CH 4 written by George C. Wilson Jan 28 1973. The article talked about the US military blunders in Vietnam.

Seems like someone re-read the article too, because some of the advice we've heeded in the Middle East.

The article claims the reserves should have been called up to fight in Vietnam before draftees. This has been done in the Middle East. The author goes on to tell about how Vietnam had no clear objective, did not have the people behind it and was fought as a "half war" we never really gave it all we had. We never mobilized as a nation for it.

We have not, as a nation, mobilized for the Middle East either but we (our president) has struggled and won the moral backing of the majority of Americans and we are, at least in appearance, going in with everything we have.

We've sent soldiers in tremendous numbers, supplies to support them, and virtually every weapon in the US inventory.

The most interesting aspect of the article I noticed was the things we haven't heeded or learned from the Vietnam experience.

First, overuse or incorrect use and reliance on airpower. From 1966 to 1972 the US dropped more explosives on Southeast Asia than all the bombs dropped in World War II. So much for restraint. This suggests that we could bomb Iraq for six year and still be no closer to an end to the war.

Next, the fear of American casualties. In Vietnam, the military's greatest fear was American casualties. For the officers in the field to report back with heavy casualties was looked upon as very bad. The war became a struggle just to keep your unit in tact – minimize casualties was the rule. Forget pursuing the enemy. Every American casualty was another nail in the military coffin by the resentful American public.

YANKS IN THE OUTBACK

Our preoccupation with minimizing American casualties in Iraq stinks of this same mentality. I believe we cannot hope to dislodge the Iraqis from Kuwait unless we are prepared to engage them. I'm not suggesting we hit them with a frontal cavalry charge but I am certain it will take bloody ground combat to rid Kuwait of the Iraqi occupiers.

In the American civil war President Lincoln never criticized Gen Grant for his high casualty rates – instead he praised him for his ability to give the North a taste of victory.

Lincoln had disdain for Gen McClellan who would not engage the army for his all-encompassing fear of taking casualties. Lincoln seemed to understand; when soldiers are committed to battle they may die.

Grant understood this. McClellan never seemed to come to grips with this fact. Grant brought the north victory, McClellan did not. McClellan was clearly superior in minimizing casualties although what that did for the union cause, I don't know.

Our overriding preoccupation with minimizing American casualties in Iraq may be our eventual downfall. Seems to me Kuwait is like Vicksburg – take it, and your losses and be done with it.

Where are General Grant and President Lincoln when you need them?

Letters to the front
18 Feb 1991 Monday

Wrote two letters to the Middle East tonight. One to my brother John and one to my cousin Richard.

Going to the States
19 Feb 1991 Tuesday

I'm going on temporary duty to the United States for three weeks leaving this Sunday. I plan to do a lot of reading on the plane. Also a lot of writing. I'm going over to review contract proposals for the Technical Services Support Contract currently awarded to TRW. Companies are bidding on the contract and I'm going back to review these proposals.

Hopefully, I'll get a lot written in this book. It will be interesting now for me to get a viewpoint of the war from the back home perspective.

Ground War about to start
21 Feb 1991 Thursday

All reports from the news are about the ground war and when it will begin. They're predicting it'll happen soon.

I read Fred Reed's column in the Air Force Times today and he made some interesting comments. Seems like he was especially inspired this time. He's complaining, as all the media, about the lack of information the military is letting out to the press and public. (at the end he finally points out – when it comes to PR, the military is a bunch of bone heads!)

His main point (I think – sometimes he wanders) is – will the higher ranking military officers (Lt Col, Maj) be in the field fighting with the troops or will they all be watching the war from a desk or high in a helicopter safe from danger?

He brings up a good point. Soldiers can't be pushed into battle, they must be lead. If the soldiers aren't lead they won't fight. They may act like their fighting but they won't have their heart in it. They won't be inspired and the first chance they have to duck out, they will – it's only human nature.

Patriotism can only take an army so far – strong and effective leadership will take that same army to victory. Leadership – that enigma. Hard to define; but everyone recognizes it; everyone's seen it, everyone's felt its power. I'm reminded of something I believe General Patton said, 'An army of sheep lead by a lion will crush an army of lions lead by a sheep!'

I hope we've got lions leading our soldiers.

Russians Getting Involved
22 Feb 1991 Friday

The Russians and Hussein appear to have worked out some sort of a peace agreement and now the US must do some quick thinking.

To go along with any such agreement is a double edged sword. Going along would allow the US to appear serious in their bid for peace. Going along will also give Hussein the breathing room he needs to try the whole thing over again at a later date.

All this talk about when the ground war will begin is driving me nuts! What the hell is a ground war?

They say "the air war will continue ... we aren't sure when the ground war will begin ..." What is all this air war / ground war talk?

As I see it, it's unadulterated Bullshit! As far as I'm concerned, after the 15th of Jan, the "baton" should have been handed over to the military commanders to carry out the objectives set by the UN council. All resources available should have been at the disposal of the field commanders to use as they see fit. Obtain the stated objectives.

How can the president claim he's letting the military run the show when the military is saying they're waiting on the president's decision to launch the ground war?

In my mind, you cannot fight a war as if the ground war and the air war are separate entities. They are not. To me that would be like playing football and telling the other team you're always going to throw; no running game.

A concerted air and ground attack from the start might have removed the Iraqi army from Kuwait by now.

Traveling to LA

25 Feb 1991 Monday (1400hrs)

I'm at the Sydney International Airport waiting for my flight that leaves at 1500 hrs for Los Angeles. My final destination is C Springs Colo for a trivial review board of some satellite technical services support contract proposals.

There's a war going on and I'm back in the states reviewing contract proposals.

Two years ago I told a Lt Col "my greatest fear is that this country will go off to war and leave me behind!"

Well, it happened.

I was back home last Aug for my twin brother's wedding. The deployment for the Middle East was underway and my younger cousin asked the very embarrassing question, "You're in the military, aren't you – how come you're not in the Middle East?"

I confidently answered this macho shattering question with, "First of all, I'm not in the military; I'm in the Air Force! Second, they want to keep this operation respectable so I wasn't invited!"

Good for a few laughs but really, I cannot figure for the life of me why I'm not there. I'll never understand why the military maintains officers who are not trained or expected to know anything about war. As an engineer, the work I do could easily be done by a civilian, freeing me up for a more combat related specialty or engineering task (combat engineer). If the Air Force has no combat positions for me then I should either be relieved or I should be let go to another branch of service.

The idea is to get rid of all these "peacetime only" personnel. Seems to me, the support roles; satellite operations, research and development, procurement etc. could all be performed by civilians.

Full time military personnel who continue to go about their mundane duties, with no direct involvement in the war effort, should probably be removed from the active duty roster – justification as not needed.

The military should not be an employment agency or an equal opportunity employer. I like what a friend of mine once said about military service, "I look at it as a calling."

Arriving in USA – Ground War Success

25 Feb 1991 Monday (13:30 LA Time)

I'm sitting in the United Airlines terminal at LAX waiting for my connecting flight to Denver. Since I've hit the American continent I've been "bombarded" with the Gulf War. All the newspapers carry the war on their headlines. The USA Today, New York Times and, I believe, The Daily (LA paper) all had a picture of Iraqi POWs marching in the front of soldiers and machines of the 2nd Marine Division my cousin Richard's gang.

The LA Times did not carry the picture, I figured because the 2nd Marines are out of the East Coast. LA's beloved are the 1st Marine Division based out of Camp Pendleton.

YANKS IN THE OUTBACK

I caught an hour's worth of news at the LAX USO. The news was saturated with reports from, about, and concerning the Gulf War – especially the allied ground advance.

All reports from the front indicate blazing success. The allied ground forces are meeting little resistance and taking minimal casualties. 14,000 Iraqi POWs were taken in the first 24 hrs – so the reports go.

The news also gave word of an Iraqi Scud missile attack on an American compound in Saudi Arabia causing extensive damage and killing many.

The USA today says the 1st and 2nd marine divisions are driving up the southern leg of Kuwait toward Kuwait City. I hope Richard is ok. He's probably shooting up the Kuwaiti countryside with his 55 caliber machine gun.

He doesn't actually fire the weapon, he directs the fire. He rides in the jeep carrying the machine gun. He's a corporal now so he's moved up to where he's the jeep commander, so to speak. He runs the show for that particular weapon system.

The military leaders are indicating they don't want to become euphoric over the initial success of the ground campaign. I think this is wise. Euphoria of this nature passed on and permeated throughout the soldiers could be devastating. An army saturated with over confidence could be routed by a strong Iraqi counterstroke. An overconfident army could lead to a breakdown in discipline. An undisciplined army is ripe to retreat in the face of a determined attack or counterattack. An army in chaotic retreat is a shopping spree, a blank check, a turkey shoot for the attackers.

The allies must be prepared for a strong Iraqi counterattack until the war's end and not before.

Allied Forces Trouncing Iraqi Army
26 Feb 1991 Tuesday

All news accounts say the allied forces are destroying the Iraqi army. Seems like it's just a matter of time before they're all defeated.

I still say we should avoid euphoria, although virtually all of Kuwait, according to reports, has been freed of Iraqi soldiers.

Reports of big tank battles between allied and Iraqis in southeastern Iraq (just north of Kuwait)

I wonder how my young cousin Richard is doing – I hope he's alright.

War Over
27 Feb 1991 Wednesday

President Bush came on the TV tonight and told the nation that the American forces will cease hostilities tonight at midnight (NY time?) Everyone is celebrating the allied victory – total victory over Saddam Hussein's Iraqi military might.

I was saying, over Maj Bob O'Shea's house tonight, that it took our ground forces to finally get the Iraqis to surrender.

The other guys in the room did not agree with me. They're all Air Force guys. Lt Steve Elliston, Maj Keven Attenhoer and Bob. They said it was the bombing that did it. I told them I was afraid people were going to draw that conclusion.

Fact – the Iraqi army did not surrender until allied ground forces went in.

I have a sneaking suspicion the battle for the peace will be much more difficult than the battle for Kuwait!

Victory Bug
1 Mar 1991 Friday

Talked to my Dad on the phone tonight. I told him I am keeping a diary about the war and that some of what I wrote may appear ridiculous in light of the tremendous success of our military – with the complete defeat of the Iraqi forces.

I know very well that "nothing succeeds like success." To criticize the Desert Storm operation is to be a "sore sport." The total collapse of the Iraqi army in the face of the allied onslaught was amazing. I was shocked. My hat is off to our military commanders and to President Bush and of course to all the military members involved.

I mentioned my concern that we might not interpret the lessons of this war properly – we may attribute the victory to all the wrong things. My greatest fear is the interpretation that air power won the war and that air power alone can win future wars.

My father said the "Fly Boys" deserve a lot of credit. I agree.

I'm still concerned our nation has come to the conclusion that the air force is all we need.

It is my firm belief that the role of the soldier never diminishes. Without soldiers, you cannot win against a determined opponent.

My heart will always go out to the soldier.

Another concern of mine is that we, as a nation, will get bitten by the "victory bug" and use the military more often and with less caution to solve our differences with other nations. An all-volunteer force makes it easier for the president to launch into adventure abroad without an immediate and violent uproar from the general populous. Volunteers go, they don't ask questions.

I read a good article by Senator U. McCarthy on this very subject (today's paper).

Troop Support

3 Mar 1991 Sunday

I read the local Colorado Springs paper "Gazette Telegraph" this morning. Very pro-military paper for this pro-military town.

Articles talk about experts such as Kennedy, McNamara, Crowe who testified before congress about the tremendous American casualties resulting from a ground war with Iraq ... how these men were "dead" wrong ... how they should not be referred to as experts ... how they should be held accountable for their misguided predictions.

Also articles on SDI (Strategic Defense Initiative), troop reductions after the war and winners and losers in the Gulf War. All pro-military.

You don't have to travel very far in this town to see support for the troops. The 7-11 store across the street from the Hotel (Red Lion Inn, Circle and I-25) has a big sign proclaiming support for the troops. The Red Lion also has a sign supporting the troops – on the marque. Most waitresses/waiters in town are wearing buttons proclaiming support for the troops.

It truly is a wonderful feeling to know people care.

God Bless Guam
3 Mar 1991 Sunday (1900 hrs)

I just had a very interesting conversation with an ex-GI in the hotel gym locker room. His name is Gerome (black man) and he used to be in the 82nd airborne division. He served in Vietnam from 1968-1970. Now he works in North Carolina for the Marine Corps in the Traffic Management Office (TMO).

He talked about his experience in Vietnam. He said there were bad times over there but he remembers the good times and the good friends he made.

He surprised me by saying the United States talks out of both sides of its mouth sometimes. He said he was fighting a case at work for a Guamanian – the military doesn't want to provide the normal benefits because Guam is not a state.

Gerome said the US fought Iraq because Iraq tried to annex Kuwait, well that's the very thing the US tried and succeeded with Guam and Puerto Rico. (I added the Philippines and Cuba!) He said the percentage of Guamanians serving in the Gulf is the greatest of any state in the union. (God bless Guam!)

I told him the Guamanians (Chamorros) are known as fighters. I told him the story of the Spanish Galleon that crashed off the shores of Guam and the survivors swam towards the shore; but the Chammorros, instead of saving the Spaniards – killed them. Not the traditional friendly natives we always hear about!

I also said one thing I've noticed/observed about Guamanians is their Patriotism – I've never seen people so proud of the fact that they are Americans. For an island nestled in the cradle of the oriental pacific – that's pretty impressive.

Gerome said they were giving this GI a hard time because Guam is not a state and therefore falls under different guidance. Probably means the GI is going to get screwed. Pretty pathetic considering, based on population, a higher percentage of Guamanians were fighting for the US in the Middle East than were soldiers from any state in the union. God bless Guam!

War Victory Speech
6 Mar 1991 Wednesday

The president (Bush) just delivered his "Gulf War Victory Speech." I could feel the electricity emanating from the congressional chamber as everyone basked in the glory of the great American victory. The president said American soldiers will not remain in the region as a permanent force but the US will continue to maintain a naval presence in the Gulf and will participate in joint military exercises with other nations.

He congratulated the soldiers and airman who pulled off the campaign. He also congratulated Sec of Defense Dick Cheney and Gens Powell and Schwarzkopf.

I'm grateful and happy for our quick and decisive victory over Iraq but I'm skeptical about our ability to handle the success. Rudyard Kipling's poem "IF" comes to mind ...

'If you can meet both triumph and disaster and treat those two imposters just the same.'

Continued US Presence in the Middle East
7 Mar 1991 Thursday

The continued US military presence in the Middle East is what concerns me. The naval presence and the joint exercise participation. I don't mind the joint exercise part as much as long as it truly is a joint exercise and not just a politically handy name to cover up US domination in the region.

One clear indication of a true joint exercise would be for every nation to participate and to pay all their own expenses. If the US foots the bill for the whole thing, then I will be very skeptical about joint exercises in the region.

Our continued naval presence in the Persian Gulf and the Middle East region smacks of greed. When we say peace in the region we say a peace acceptable to the US. A peace that includes the free flow of oil to western and western sympathizing nations at a price acceptable to the US.

The president says a stable Middle East is of vital importance to the US national security. Sometimes our mentality appears ludicrous. We speak of peace even if the Arab world has to live under the thumb of western powers. Hell, the early Americans went to war with their own mother country (England) over a tiny little tea tax! You could hardly call that domination or oppression. As a matter of fact, I was doing some reading on our revolutionary war and discovered a big reason for the war was that a lot of Americans were in debt. A good way to get out of debt is to go to war, defeat the people/government you owe, and there you are – out of debt!

I don't disagree with the colonial Americans at all – I admire their courage and fortitude. I do disagree with our present American policies which appear to tell the world – we don't care if you live in oppression or poverty – as long as we continue to get what we want. The national resources we need, the products we need, the food we need …

We were talking the other day at work how our government (military, Space Command) spend so much money and usually in a wasteful manner. We were joking that "The Air Force will spare no expense to save money!" and "The Air Force is going to save money, no matter how much it costs!"

Well, the same line of reasoning appears to come from our government concerning peace "We will maintain peace in the region no matter how many people we have to kill in order to achieve it!"

Soldier's Welcome Home

8 Mar 1991 Friday (0600 hrs)

The first soldiers have returned home from the Middle East. Soldiers from the 24th Mechanized Division out of Georgia. What a site to see! Very heartwarming to see the soldiers reunited with their families; to see husbands and wives, children and parents, friends and loved ones all reunited. Beautiful.

I'm trying to place myself in their shoes, thinking how much joy they must feel. I'm happy for them all.

One TV clip showed a soldier hugging an Asian lady and this particular image tugged at my heart. The lady, who looked Filipina, was showing her emotion, her uncontrollable emotion – hugging the soldier with everything she had, eyes closed and tears falling.

AF Academy Boxing

8 Mar 1991 Friday (2200 hrs)

I went to the AF Academy Field House tonight to watch cadet boxing. I was invited by my friend Maj Bob O'Shea. He was one of the judges. Also, when he was a cadet '79' he won this very same boxing competition for his weight class.

I was surprised when I got to the field house. I wasn't expecting the event to be so grand. The place was packed. The arena was dark except for the ring. The crowd was noisy and they screamed and yelled even louder every time a good punch landed.

I was impressed – those boys can fight. Good quality boxing.

Feeling of Patriotism

9 Mar 1991 Saturday

The feeling of patriotism is everywhere in C Springs. American flags are everywhere. Cars have them on the antennas, windows, bumpers dashboards. Flags wave from many houses, stores, and businesses.

I imagine the feeling has permeated throughout the USA. All the college basketball players have an American flag patch sewn to their uniforms. The pro baseball players are talking about putting on American flag decals or painting on their helmets (or uniform, somewhere – I forget where now that I have to write it down!)

Also, since victory the politicians are at it. They're bitching back and forth about what to do with those who voted against the decision to use force in the Gulf.

I think all this finger pointing is a waste of time. I personally think all of Congress is guilty just by virtue of their position! If they happened to vote the right way it was purely by accident. It is a sad statement, but unfortunately politicians do no vote for what is right but for what they think will get them reelected.

Not all Rosy on the Farm
13 Mar 1991 Wednesday

From the news reports, all is not rosy on our Middle Eastern farm. Iraqi rebels are rising up against Hussein's troops. In Kuwait, the people don't have enough food; there's no electricity, power and basic supplies.

The "Grand Poo Bah" of Kuwait is due to return home today and I'm sure he'll get an earful from his people. They are demanding more democratic reforms.

Apparently, the Saudi's will pressure the Kuwaiti King to maintain strict control over the people.

Heading Back to Oz
15 Mar 1991 Friday

I'm on my way to Australia. First leg, Denver to LA. My trip to the states has been enlightening and I'm looking forward to returning in May and reporting to Wright-Patterson in June. I've already got my follow-on assignment to Wright Laboratory.

I just put down a book titled "The Parameters of Military Ethics" edited by Mathew and Brown. I bought it at Peterson AFB.

The book takes on a very difficult subject. Some of the opinions expressed are very enlightening but after reading a number of essays, I have become slightly unmotivated. (I believe the study of ethics should be mandatory among military personnel.)

I find the essays to be somewhat dry. They don't rip you apart at the guts. Yes, one article mentions the My Lai massacre but in a very academic manner, as if nobody really got hurt, just some ethics got mixed up.

Overall the book serves a very useful purpose but as a tool to help motivate military personnel to examine their ethical standing, I don't know how much effect it will have. I would guess little – too dull!

Talking about ethics is good, but forcing someone to experience the human gut-wrenching tug of ethical dilemma is a better tool for getting someone to examine their moral innards.

A great literary source for such gut-wrenching is found in fiction. I never understood the value of fiction until I read "Killer Angels" a book about the civil war battle at Gettysburg. It's a fictional account and portrayal of some of the key figures in that fateful campaign.

The author takes the factual evidence to paint a realistic picture of the human side of Gettysburg – the conflict between the Generals, the human suffering of the soldiers as they fall from cannon fire and the psychological impacts on the soldiers delivering the devastating and deadly fire.

The fictional account takes us beyond the dry facts. It takes us beyond the factual numbers and documentary pictures. It takes us beyond observations and places us in the confrontation. We are there. Fiction, well written, drives the point home.

The Killer Angels was mandatory reading for my brother John at West Point. It's good to know our future military leaders are reading such material.

Another masterpiece of fiction is "The Red Badge of Courage."

Books such as these can be used as the basis for ethical discussions. Did a certain character act ethically? Would you do the same thing? Was Lee wrong to order Pickett's charge?

A dry book on military ethics will never stir the inner core of the human spirit; not like a well written story – fact or fiction - that brings the reader into the very depths of the conflict at hand.

Headquarters Wants Blood!

18 Mar 1991 Monday

My first day back in the office and I got the disappointing news.

Capt Connie Jefferson ran into my office this morning short of breath, "Did you hear what happened to Capt Marcus? Headquarters wants his head on a platter! You know that SCUD that hit the barracks? Well, Capt Marcus was on duty and sent it out low speed. It didn't meet the criteria but they're criticizing him for not sending it high speed! These guys are crazy! By headquarters own rules he couldn't send it high speed – it didn't meet the criteria. He knew it was a launch but he didn't want to get decertified so he sent it low speed. He did his job. They want him dead. They're looking for scapegoats; Capt Marcus is first on their list. The DO and Commander are in trouble too. The whole site looks bad. Our reputation is mud. It's a mess."

I was taken aback by Connie's barrage. It was a bit much for me to digest all at once. But, I was able to work out two things - Connie was upset and Capt Marcus was in big trouble.

The SCUD missile launch that hit the barracks has been the preoccupying news at site since I left for the US. It happened on 26 Feb at about 02:30 local Woomera time.

Normally Capt Marcus works days – he's the Training Dept Chief – but that night he was the on-duty crew commander. And, his deputy happened to be Capt Frentani. These are the two most conservative guys we have. Both are very concerned about their careers; number one priority – don't make any mistakes. Bad combination if you're looking for bold action.

The DO called another meeting today to re-hash all the facts. I attended.

As I entered the conference room I could sense the seriousness of the situation. First of all, the room was packed; standing room only. I'd never seen this many people in the conference room for a meeting. I slid down the wall squeezing in with the others standing up.

The room carried an awkward silence as everyone stared blankly at the floor or the wall while waiting. There was one empty chair at the head of the conference table; opposite the DO. It was reserved; no one dared sit there. We all knew it was reserved; not so much a position of importance but more like the seat for the condemned man.

The awkward silence built until he finally walked into the room.

As he entered, Capt Marcus started for the wall like the rest of us, but the DO yelled out, "Sit over here Capt. This seat is reserved for you!" Capt Marcus shifted quickly trying to make it look like he was going to sit there all along. I could tell he was putting on a brave face. I felt for him and wanted him to come out of this looking good. Inside, I was cheering for him.

Capt Frentani stood up against the wall quietly in the back of the room.

The DO kicked it off, "Ok, Capt Marcus tell us again what happened during that launch?"

Capt Marcus explained it so even I could understand. Here's a summary of his explanation.

He knew it was a SCUD launch. He knew because it came out of Iraq and it was "bright" enough for a launch and they'd seen launches like this on training tapes so it was familiar. But, on the training tapes you can be wrong and it's no big deal, but during a real launch you have to be right; after all, that's the direction all the crew commanders have received – don't send high speed unless you're 100 percent sure it's a launch! And, to further that direction headquarters added the caveat – don't send high speed unless the computer data meets all the launch criteria. And, that's what drove his decision to send low speed – the computer data did not meet launch criteria. So, by headquarters direction, he was prevented from sending it via high speed message.

The DO wanted more, "How come it didn't meet high speed criteria?"

Capt Marcus started to answer but Karl Henry from Aerojet put up his hand, "I can answer that sir."

Capt Marcus was more than happy to turn this question over to Karl.

"Ok, Karl, let's have it."

"The online computer was on Flight 12. It turns out the direction the missile was launched is a poor viewing geometry for Flight 12;

it's coming right down the barrel of the satellite. As such the computer can't pick up good motion. Without good motion, the computer won't give you the criteria needed for sending high speed."

"So, the data didn't support a high speed send, is that right?"

Karl confirmed what the DO asserted, "That's right sir. It didn't meet high speed criteria. The TAI (tactical assessment index) was only 40. We can't send with a TAI that low."

"Could he have sent it high speed anyway?"

Karl offered his opinion, "Yes, he could have sent it high speed but technically he would be breaking the headquarters rules. We all know it's a launch but what do you do? Do you send high speed and break the rules or do you follow the rules?

The DO started to vent.

"Well, it turns out we can't win here at site. We follow their rules and look what happens? Headquarters still wants our head on a platter. They want to know why we didn't send this launch high speed and they don't want any excuses. They're saying we should have sent it high speed – there's no defense for not doing it. They don't care about computer criteria or sufficient data or anything. They're fuming!"

The DO continued his monologue.

"If headquarters feels this way then they should have told us; they should have changed the rules. They should have allowed us to send anything we see in Iraq via high speed then they can sort it out. That's what the army commanders were asking for – send it all; let them decide if it's real or not. But, headquarters is still in the cold war mindset looking for ballistic missiles and can't tolerate any mistakes – zero defects mentality. And, now they're crying because we followed their stupid rules."

The DO floated a question for the group, "What about Flight 15? Did we see the launch on the offline computer?"

"Yes!" came a chorus from several people in the jammed packed room.

"And ....?" Questioned the DO.

Karl wrestled the floor again and gave the explanation. Karl is the recognized site mission expert and has been analyzing and studying both the offline and online data to figure out what happened.

"Flight 15 had a great view of the launch. If Flight 15 was on-line it would have gone out high speed. The computer built a great launch report and the crew commanders would have all criteria met allowing them to confidently send it out high speed. But, unfortunately, the online computer was on Flight 12 which had a really bad view; it's looking at the missile head on and therefore didn't show good motion; the TAI was crap; too low to meet high speed release criteria."

Capt Marcus chimed in, "Sir, I had Capt Frentani and a Sgt Walker on the offline computer and they verified it was a launch. Then we had a short discussion about headquarters guidance and decided to send low speed. Headquarters guidance doesn't say anything about what we see on the offline computer. It's pretty blunt guidance – no false reports – ever. Only send high speed if all criteria is met – no exceptions. We followed the headquarters guidance. God knows I wanted to send it high speed. But, I didn't want to get decertified either. I saw what happened to Lt Kelly when he sent a high speed launch report based on data from the "hot shadow" satellite. Look what headquarters did to him; they had no mercy."

He was referring Lt Kelly decertification story I mentioned before. Lt Kelly got it right – it was a launch. He used the "hot shadow" computer to verify it was a valid launch; this is against HQ rules. The DO congratulated him for taking brave, bold and brilliant action. But, headquarters overruled the DO and ordered LT Kelly decertified for breaking their rules. Now, headquarters is asking for Capt Marcus' head on a platter for following their rules!

Apparently, HQ is getting a ton of heat from the battlefield commanders. Now, HQ is looking for a scapegoat. Looks like they've found their man in Capt Marcus.

HQ wanted us to operate on a peacetime – cold war – mentality. They couldn't see clear to introduce some flexibility. For instance, they could have given the OK for us to send anything and everything out of the Middle East area. No questions asked, just send it all – HIGH SPEED. Then let the battlefield commanders decide what's what. But, no - HQ is holding on dearly to its cold war mission. No flexibility; no way to make adjustments; no creative thinking.

Seems like the real HQ mission is to have no false reports.

Mission accomplished.

Dave Ives

HQ changes the rules!
19 Mar 1991 Tuesday

The DO was not happy when he read the message we received from HQ last night giving us new direction. It's too late and it's laughable. They're telling us to close the gate but the horse has already bolted!

The Gulf War is over. And, now they tell us to take a wartime approach.

The message directs us to send all, any and everything we see in the Middle East area via high speed message. This is in support of the "war-fighters." Apparently, after the barracks debacle, the ground commanders demanded we stop all this "chicken shit" cold war "zero defects" crap and start sending everything. Even though HQ can't live with false reports, apparently, the warfighters can.

The message is clear, if we see something, anything – even a dust speck on the computer screen – and it's in the Middle East area – SEND, SEND, SEND – HIGH SPEED.

Unfortunately for the war-fighters, HQ just got around to officially notifying us to adapt this new direction.

This is what we should have done from day one. This is what I'd call a wartime footing. But, unfortunately, this sort of thing probably happens in every war. It takes a certain amount of time to transition from the peacetime military to the wartime military. Hopefully, you don't lose too many soldiers – or the war – during this transition period.

Capt Marcus Decertified

20 Mar 1991 Wednesday

Capt Marcus and Capt Frentani were officially decertified today. I saw them on the ops floor undergoing retraining. They looked dejected. Their trainer looked dejected. The crew looked dejected.

But, this isn't the normal decertification dejected look. It's more of a look that says, "What are we training for if HQ is just going to change the rules on us whenever it suits them; whenever they need a convenient scapegoat?"

HQ was a bad word around here before; now it's even worse.

Crew morale has hit a new low point.

Dances with Wolves

1 Apr 1991 Monday

I'm in Adelaide SA at the Adelaide International Motel ANZAC Highway.

Got up early this morning 0400 hrs, took Lt Kelly to the airport . He's off to a new assignment in Darwin. I'll miss him and his bold approach to life.

I picked up a copy of "The Australian" (newspaper) and read some interesting news about our Gulf exploits. Seems there is a rift afloat between our boys in Washington and our boys in the field. Gen Schwarzkopf says he was ordered to stop fighting in the Gulf before he could adequately destroy Hussein's army. I suppose the general would like to support the Rebels trying to overthrow Hussein but Washington strictly forbids it. The general figures if he had destroyed the Iraqi army completely the rebels wouldn't be in the mess they're in. Apparently many civilians are being slaughtered in the fighting.

President Bush and Defense Secretary (Cheney) are claiming everyone was in on the decision to end the allied onslaught in the Gulf. General Schwarzkopf claims he was just informed of the decision and carried out the order. All this according to the papers.

The best part of the day came when I went and saw the movie "Dances with Wolves." Excellent! Took my breath away – my idea of a movie. Majestic scenes. Wonderful story. Well told.

The portrayal of the Sioux Indians was magic. The trust and bonding built up throughout the story between the cavalry soldier John Dunbar "Dances with Wolves" and the Sioux is fantastic and left me longing for such a relationship.

Our culture & society does not facilitate such bonding. Ours is – 'everybody look out for yourself – independence – I don't need anybody, I can make it on my own.'

We are social animals with an inner desire to belong and to be needed and to be appreciated and to fill a distinct role in our family, group, class society – call it what you will.

Our technology world seems to be moving us farther and farther away from this simple fact. As we move farther away from it the more we crave it – belonging, fitting in, having a purpose within the group.

The Sioux portrayed in the movie had it. Everyone fit in, had a role, was needed. They even found a place for the white man when he demonstrated his ability to act civilized and adapt to the ways of the Sioux!

For me the most moving part of the story came near the end, when "Dances with Wolves" is leaving the Sioux tribe, when the Indian on the horse at the top of the cliff yelled out throughout the canyon "Dances with Wolves is my friend!"

The scene moved me to tears because when the Sioux said "friend" he meant something much more powerful than what it means to us today. He meant it with his whole being. He would lay down his life for Dances with Wolves. "Friend" as in brother, as in blood, as in body, as in soul. Oh we all long for such friendship! Oh what joy to those who find it!

THE END

Share your insights, reflections and feedback. Write a heartfelt review on amazon.com and/or goodreads.com.

EPILOGUE

Inconvenient Fact

There's a big glaring inconvenient fact that spoils any official Air Force investigation claim that the JDFN (Woomera) operations crews were at fault in carrying out their duties during the SCUD missile barracks tragedy.

FACT: All three Defense Support Program (DSP) satellite tracking sites – Buckley in Denver, Kapaun in Germany and Woomera in Australia detected the 26 February 1991 "barracks" SCUD missile in real time yet not one of them reported the event as a valid missile launch via the high speed reporting channels.

This fact is spelled out on pages 169 and 179 of the book "America's Space Sentinels – The History of the DSP and SBIRS Satellite Systems" by Jeffrey T. Richelson.

You mean to tell me there's a war going on, the sites see moving infrared data coming from the war zone – something that's probably a SCUD missile launch – and yet all three sites make the same incredible decision – don't send?

Why didn't all three sites come to the more logical conclusion – send it high speed? No discussion, no big decision process, no-brainer – SEND!

There's only one conclusion that makes any sense. There's only one conclusion that would explain why all three missile warning sites made the same call.

What's common to all three sites?

Answer: Headquarters.

Where do the sites get their orders, direction and guidance for missile warning procedures?

Answer: Headquarters

So, here's the only reasonable and logical conclusion –

The sites were still operating under peacetime, cold war, missile warning rules per headquarters direction.

And, the overriding peacetime, cold war, missile warning rule was this – *no false reports.* Not allowed; not tolerated; not good for your military career.

Unfortunately this rule was not a good fit for wartime operations in the First Gulf War.

Thought Experiment

Let's do a thought experiment to uncover how this event could have come about; this bizarre event that seems to defy common sense. After all, the more logical result would have been for all three crews - at all three sites - to send out a "high speed" missile warning message.

What was going on – at a systemic level – that would lead to the exact opposite result?

Well, let's start by asking a basic question, *"What direction did headquarters give the missile warning sites?"*

I don't know, but remember, this is a thought experiment so we can introduce some concepts.

How about if we do this – let's come up with two extreme cases. Then from these two extreme cases we pick the one that most closely explains the "do not send" response from the sites. This will represent our "flawed" case – the wrong guidance. Therefore by default, the correct headquarters direction should have leaned toward our other extreme case.

Headquarters Direction to the Missile Warning Sites

Extreme Case Number 1:

Hey guys, there's a war going on in the Middle East, so we're changing the rules ... anything you see in that area send it out high speed. Don't worry about getting it wrong – don't worry about false reports – don't worry about getting decertified. The cold war rules about false reports apply elsewhere but for the Middle East – you guys have a "get out of jail free" card – we'll take the heat for any false reports coming out of the war zone. So, bottom line, you see something in the war zone – anything – could be a speck of dust on your computer screen – send it high speed – SEND; SEND; SEND! If you're wrong, don't worry. As long as it's out of the Middle East war zone, we won't decertify you.

Extreme Case Number 2:

Just because there's a war going on doesn't give you any excuse for sending false reports. You send out a false report and we'll have you decertified – you get it wrong and we'll have your head. So here's the rule – if you're not sure – if the missile warning report doesn't meet our strict "release" criteria then don't send it high speed. Our goal – your goal – NO FALSE REPORTS - NONE!

Since all three crews at the three different sites came to the same conclusion – "don't send high speed", which of the two extreme cases above do you feel best fits the headquarters direction handed down to the missile warning sites?

I agree with you – headquarters gave direction that leaned toward our extreme case number 2. That would explain the "don't send" decision from all three crews at all three sites. Case 2 is our "flawed case."

Now, as part of our thought experiment, let's ask another question that should shed some much needed light on this whole tragic affair.

If headquarters had given direction to the sites per our extreme case number 1 above, do you suppose the response from the three missile warning sites would have been different?

Do you suppose maybe at least one of the sites would have sent a high speed missile warning message?

Or – maybe even more likely – do you suppose all three crews at all three sites would have sent out high speed warning messages?

I believe our thought experiment has done its job.

But, I'll leave you to be the judge.

ABOUT THE AUTHOR

Dave Ives joined the US Air Force in October 1981 and served as a medic in the military hospital at Mather AFB near Sacramento California until early 1984. Then he attended Ohio State University under an active duty commissioning program graduating with a degree in aerospace engineering. In July 1987, Dave reported to Buckley Air National Guard Base near Denver and joined the satellite systems engineering team. In early 1990, he volunteered for a 15 month assignment to the Joint Defense Facility Nurrungar (JDFN) in outback South Australia.

Dave now resides in Alice Springs, Northern Territory Australia.

For more about Dave, visit his website: ivesguy.com.

Other books by Dave Ives:

> Live Free or Die
> Dreams of the Philippines
> Perception is Reality
> Working my BUT Off! *Reflections of a Property Investor.*

Printed in Great Britain
by Amazon